SHUSAKU ENDO

The Girl I Left Behind

TRANSLATED BY MARK WILLIAMS

A NEW DIRECTIONS BOOK

Manufactured in the United States of America
New Directions Books are printed on acid-free paper
First published clothbound by New Directions in 1995
Published by arrangement with Peter Owen Publishers, London

Library of Congress Cataloging-in-Publication Data

Endō, Shūsaku, 1923–
    [Watashi ga suteta onna, English]
    The girl I left behind / Shusaku Endo ; translated by Mark
Williams.
        p.   cm.
    ISBN 0-8112-1303-X
    I. Williams, Mark.   II. Title
PL849.N4W313   1995
895.6'35—dc20   95-11038
                                                                     CIP

New Directions Books are published for James Laughlin
by New Directions Publishing Corporation
80 Eighth Avenue, New York 10011

The Girl I Left Behind

My diary (1)

Maggots plague the unaffiliated man

I know it sounds rather hackneyed, but I wonder how many of you modest female readers have had the opportunity of looking in on an apartment inhabited by two young men. Without doing so, you can have no idea how lazy they are and can never have experienced at first hand the absolute chaos and stench of their living quarters. But I should like to suggest to all of you with a brother or a boy-friend who is living away from home pursuing his studies that one day you carry out a surprise attack on his apartment. The moment you slide open the door, you will let out an involuntary shriek, turn bright red and then be left speechless.

This story begins some three years after the end of the war in the apartment of two young men. I realize there may be certain sections that will cause my female readers to wince, but that is not altogether my fault. At the time, Nagashima Shigeo and I, Yoshioka Tsutomu, were students enjoying our bachelor existences. The Kanda apartment we shared may not quite have been maggot-infested, but in the summer we took pride in the number of fleas jumping about all over the place. In this period of severe housing shortage, it was no easy matter to locate a six-mat room which overlooked the burnt-out ruins and recently restored makeshift shelters of Kanda, especially one for which no deposit or key money was required.

The name of my friend, Nagashima Shigeo, may well conjure up images of the famous baseball player of the day, but I must avoid giving the impression of a sturdy, tough and generally rather smart youth. The ribs that could be clearly seen through his skinny frame were testimony both to the problems of eking out an existence as an impoverished student and to the fact that, for a long time, he had had to make do with eating nothing but *zōsui*[1] and cheap fish. But I was even worse. Having contracted a mild form of polio as a child, I was extremely thin and still somewhat restricted in the movement of my right leg.

Neither of us was particularly diligent about attending class. In view of conditions in the countryside in the immediate postwar period, we were unable to rely on regular remittances from home and, as with the vast majority of students of the time, we kept ourselves busy with part-time jobs. I call them part-time jobs, but they were a far cry from the twenty, even thirty thousand yen that the smart young students of today can earn for playing in a band or for serving on the student executive. The jobs that we found tended to involve delivering from the wholesaler to the retail outlet the electrical goods and aluminium pots that had just begun to appear on the market, selling lottery tickets and ice-creams at the velodrome or by the seaside and other such menial tasks totally out of keeping with our status as university students.

'I'm strapped for cash. I need a woman.' That is a pretty fair reflection of the thoughts that whirled around inside our heads . . . if you'll excuse the rather vulgar expressions. I hardly need tell you how short of money we were, but the young women who were widely cited along with stockings as among the first to strengthen themselves after the war, would hardly give a second thought to such impoverished students up to their eyes in part-time work.

On days when we weren't working, Nagashima and I would lie around on our unfolded bedding from which the padding protruded, constantly sighing through the masks over our mouths, 'I want some cash. I want a woman.' We used to wear masks not because we had colds, but because in a room that

1. A simple stew of rice and vegetables

hadn't seen a duster for over a month, the slightest movement used to send up clouds of dust like trails of smoke from our *futon*. Being lazy, we had no alternative but to cover our mouths with masks.

It all happened one beautiful autumn afternoon as the sunlight poured in through the cracked window. The air was so serene that the voice of Kasagi Shizuko singing a recent number was clearly audible from a radio in one of the distant houses. The two of us sat cross-legged on the bedding slurping the potato stew we had made in the electric heater and, for some unknown reason, the sweet smell of the stew mixed with the stench emanating from the bedspreads reminded me of my mother. I realized that this smell, combined with the serenity of the clear autumn sunlight that appeared to carve a great swathe through the sky, was enough to bring out the sentimental side in human nature.

'Hey, if you're not going to eat that, pass it over here, will you?' Nagashima held the china bowl he had taken from the local noodle shop to his lips and stared at me with a look of longing in his eyes.

'Get lost! I've just given you two more spoonfuls!'

'We can't go on living like this for ever. I feel I'm rotting away, both physically and mentally.' Nagashima could be surprisingly sentimental on occasions, and he broached this new subject quite out of the blue.

Apparently he had been raised in Yamanashi Prefecture where every autumn was taken up with grape-picking. He told me that the bunches of grapes on the latticed vines sparkled like deep-blue jewels in the sunlight and that young girls wearing sedge hats and gaiters spent their days throwing grapes into hand-held baskets.

'I must have been a real child, because every time the young girls reached up to pick the grapes, I used to look at the white kneecaps you could see between the bottom of their kimonos and their gaiters. I thought they were really beautiful! I don't know why, but every autumn I think of those white kneecaps.'

As he continued to eat, Nagashima seemed to be reliving

those times and I felt as though I too could picture those sprightly young girls reaching up to pick grapes under the autumn sun, their white kneecaps protruding from between their kimonos and their black gaiters. How I yearned for the chance to be able to pick grapes with them, even once.

'Oh no! I've got to go off to work.' Nagashima had awoken from a dream to confront stark reality once more. 'Never mind about girls. What we need at the moment is money.'

Standing up hurriedly, he took off his padded kimono which was coated in oil and rummaged around in the solitary old wicker basket we kept in the closet.

'They're filthy!' Like a dog foraging in the dirt, he drew out a succession of dirty vests and underpants. 'Surely there's something I can wear? The trouble is you don't wash properly even when you do take a bath.'

As a matter of fact, both Nagashima and I tended to throw our dirty clothes straight into this basket. When we had first moved in together, we had been careful to wear our own underwear, but gradually my vests had become his and his underwear had become mine. What's more, being lazy, we had acquired the bad habit of trying to save on washing by simply selecting from the pile of dirty underwear that had lain unwashed for a month those items of clothing in which the grime was not over-obtrusive. (Dear reader, please don't grimace like that. As I said just a minute ago, it's not only us, but your brothers, your boy-friends. . . . In short, virtually all men living alone are just the same.)

The sun shone weakly on Nagashima and me as we went our separate ways through the congestion in front of the station at Ochanomizu. He was off to his job which entailed exercising the dog at some mansion in the residential quarter of the city. But this was not just any old dog. According to Nagashima, the dog concerned was a pointer that lived off the most sumptuous butter and milk dishes. Even in the immediate aftermath of the war, there were still some Japanese who lived in the lap of luxury.

I got off the train at Surugadai and went to the office of the National Students' Relief Association. That may sound very grand, but in reality the place was a small makeshift affair that positively buzzed with students. But in this small office, we could find help in locating inexpensive accommodation and new part-time jobs.

There was a crowd of students absorbing the weak rays of the autumn sun in front of the office, their cheeks as sunken as mine. Some were still dressed in demobilization gear and square college caps or shabby suits, but all of these young men were students.

Joining the queue, I looked up at the list of temporary job vacancies that had been affixed to the wall of the office. *Garbage collection from the lawns in front of the Imperial Palace and at Shibaura.* There was good money involved here, but it would be tough for me with my history of polio as a child. The money to be made selling lottery tickets was paltry, given the effort involved and the vacancies for private tutoring were virtually monopolized by students from such élite centres as Tokyo University and Hitotsubashi.

I was just beginning to despair when my attention was caught by a small piece of paper that had been posted unobtrusively in the far right-hand corner of the notice-board. A red diagonal line had been drawn through all those in which students had already expressed interest, but there was no red ink to be seen on this particular one.

Location: Chiba Prefecture, Sakuramachi

Job description: Delivering publicity leaflets; some light physical work

Daily remuneration: 200 yen plus travel allowance.

The other students had no doubt spotted this notice, but had probably been put off by the thought of travelling all the way to Chiba. The idea of going to some distant rural community in Chiba on a stomach ravaged by a meagre diet of rolls and potato stew was not appealing.

Shall I? Shan't I? I tried fingering the small die I carried in my pocket. Whenever I wavered over a decision, I relied on this die. I was possessed of a wild belief in the need to entrust my destiny, not to my own will but to some external determinant, a sense of resignation that was so typical of students in those immediate post-war years. The die turned up an even number and so I went up to the window.

'Oh right, this one. This one....' The middle-aged official placed his old pen behind his ear and checked the card.

'*Swan Industrial. Kanda, Jinbōchō, Ward 3....* Hmm. This may not be a very reputable company.'

'It doesn't matter. I don't mind if it's reputable or not.'

The clerk gave a somewhat wry smile and quietly passed me the employment forms that were to be handed to the employer.

It took less than fifteen minutes to walk to Jinbōchō, Ward 3. Here I discovered one small cluster of old houses which must have been spared the ravages of war. People must have been preparing dinner because through cracks in the wooden fences I could hear the sound of firewood being cut and charcoal braziers being lit. An old man who went round performing impromptu shows using picture stories cycled slowly past me.

'Excuse me. Can you tell me how to find Swan Industrial?' I asked a middle-aged woman who was standing outside her house with a child on her back.

'Wan Industrial?'

'Not Wan, Swan. It's English for those white birds you see swimming on ponds.'

'I don't remember anything of that name around here. But if it's Block 17, it must be right behind here.'

Once more I set off through the smoke from the braziers behind the man with the picture stories. It was beginning to grow dark. The old man turned into a side-street and stopped his bicycle with a squeal of brakes in front of a dirty one-storey house that seemed at first glance to be an estate agent's.

This was Swan Industrial. Going by the name, I had pictured some white Western-style building. But nothing could have been further from the truth. The house was stained with dirt, looking for all the world like a small crow that had just crawled out of a rubbish tip. I opened the ill-fitting glass door. There was a telephone on the solitary desk that stood on the dirt floor and a man in spectacles with a page-boy haircut and loud-coloured trousers that appeared to have been passed on by the Occupation forces sat with his feet on the desk and looked me up and down as I entered.

'Kim-san, Kim-san. I'll put the goods down here.'

The old man with the picture stories put the pictures he had brought on his bicycle down on the floor. They were obviously related to the business. I surmised from his name that the man with the page-boy cut was a foreigner who had come to Tokyo after the war.

'Right, right. Are you coming again tomorrow?'

The old man nodded and left the room, causing the glass door to rattle.

'So what can I do for you?' The man with the page-boy cut stuck his finger up his nose as he spoke.

'Actually, I saw your ad. I'm a student. Here's my student i.d.'

'Right, OK. You've come from the *stutent* union, have you?'

'No, from the Students' Relief Association.'

'Right. The *chob* involves delivering publicity leaflets. You interested?'

'Yes. Just delivering publicity leaflets. Right?' Influenced by his strange pronunciation, I felt as if my own Japanese would be adversely affected.

'Those are the leaflets.' Kim-san pointed at a bundle of posters and flyers piled up in one corner of the dirt floor. He wore a large gold ring on one finger.

It appeared that my job for the following day was to walk around Sakuramachi and the neighbouring villages in Chiba Prefecture pasting up and delivering these posters. Picking one up I collected a hundred yen to cover my travelling expenses for the first couple of days and left.

The sound of a *tōfu* dealer's bugle somewhere in the distance made me feel miserable. I suddenly recalled how, only that day, Nagashima had told me over his stew how he felt dirty both physically and mentally. I looked at the flyer as I walked down the street. The paper was smeared with ink from the copy machine and contained the following carelessly written message: *The great hits of ENOKEN – the darling of Asakusa. ENOKEN of Tokyo – Now appearing in Sakuramachi.*

Even a child of three would have known the name Enoken. As the number one performer in the world of comedy active both on the screen and the stage, one would expect to find him contracted to appear at the major theatres in the six major metropolitan areas. It was inconceivable that he should bring his show to a grubby country town in Chiba Prefecture.

And what's more, even if the unbelievable were to happen and he agreed to perform in this backwater out of some philanthropic consideration, there was no chance that he would entrust the organization of such an event to Swan Industrial with its dubious-looking premises.

'There's something funny going on here.' I recalled the words of warning that the middle-aged man at the Students' Relief Association, his hair just beginning to betray traces of silver, had muttered to me: 'This may not be a very reputable company.'

But in my current situation, it made little difference to me whether this company were reputable or not. Provided I posted up those flyers in Sakuramachi, I would receive two hundred yen plus a travel allowance. That was all that mattered to me. At Suzuran Street in Kanda, availing myself of the money I had been given by that foreigner with the page-boy haircut, I enjoyed the rare treat of a bowl of *oden*[2] and some fried rice before returning home.

Nagashima must have been gadding about somewhere because there was no sign of him at home. I slipped under the bedding still permeated with the distinctive smell of body odour and, unable to sleep, found myself thinking absently about

2. Japanese hotpot

the grape-picking girls he had mentioned earlier. I was young and the thought of the white kneecaps of those young girls toiling under the autumn sun was like a fountainhead deep within my being.

At about ten o'clock the following morning I left Nagashima sleeping like an emaciated roast chicken and, putting on my old raincoat, went outside.

'What's up? You *ton't* look too *cood*. Are you OK?' Still wearing the same large ring on his finger, Kim-san of the page-boy cut pointed at the pile of flyers just as he had the previous day and said, 'Put these in that rucksack. I want you to go round the places on this piece of paper.'

It seemed that Sakuramachi was about an hour from Ichikawa by bus. My job was to travel around three or four of the neighbourhood villages handing out these flyers. That would be quite hard work. But by the time I realized that it would not be profitable on my daily allowance of two hundred yen, it was too late.

'That's quite a lot of. . . .' I ended up giving vent to my concern. 'Is the message on these flyers true?'

'Ah, ha. You *tink* it's a lie, do you?' Kim-san glanced at me through his narrow eyes and a faint smile flitted across his sunken cheeks. There was nothing more to be said.

'All right.'

'Just a minute.' Whether he was trying to win me over or had been possessed of a sense of the love of the Buddha for this pitiful student worker was hard to tell. At any rate, he placed a hand in the pocket of his gaudy trousers and handed me a pack of Lucky Strike cigarettes. Like the clothes he was wearing, he had probably bought these too on the black market from the Occupation forces.

I had thought nothing of this pile of posters and flyers, but the rucksack he lent me was surprisingly heavy on my back. As a consequence of my childhood polio, I was not particularly well suited to carrying such a load. Not surprisingly, the train from Ochanomizu to Chiba was fairly empty at this hour, but I was acutely aware that, with my rucksack, I must

15

have looked like a potato salesman. Speaking of which, there was a group of five or six delivery men, replete with old rucksacks and various other bundles of goods, in the carriage in front of me.

As I transferred to a bus at Ichikawa Station, the bus lane stretched out into the distance. One solitary pine tree stood by the side of the road. This was the Ichikawa Pine, a natural monument. The cinema sign to the side was adorned with a large ink profile of the actor Ikebe Ryō. After a while we turned left and, as we left the town, the bus began to shake. The groves of zelkova and oak trees lent the scene a distinctly autumnal air. The Japanese chestnut trees were a withered brown colour and gave no signs of life, but the leaves of the large trees glistened in the sunlight and rained down like money on the roads and farmhouse roofs.

The ploughed fields appeared black. The fallen leaves lent the thatched roofs of the farmhouses a reddish hue. The persimmons in the farmyards were indescribably beautiful. On learning from the conductor with the extravagant lipstick that we were only two stops from Sakuramachi, I jumped down from the bus.

I had already gained experience of pasting up posters and delivering flyers during the election of the previous year. Like the vast majority of students, my political affiliations lay with the revolutionary party. But ideals had to be set aside when it came to choosing a part-time job. My mentor of the time was some civil engineer-turned-conservative candidate and I had felt no qualms at all about pasting his poster that included his photograph to the lampposts of Shibuya and Sangenjaya. But now, as I opened my rucksack and threw these dubious flyers into the letter-boxes and on to the verandas of these peaceful farmhouses, I felt strangely guilty.

Everyone must have been working in the fields, because all the farmhouses appeared devoid of human habitation. A cock crowed and, startled by the sound of my footsteps, jumped up on to the balcony. There was an old magazine with a torn cover lying in the yard. I casually picked it up and began to turn the pages at random. It was a magazine called *Bright Star*, full of photographs and gossip about movie stars and pop stars. Concluding that anything left in the yard exposed to the elements in this way must be destined for the rubbish dump, I calmly slipped it into my raincoat pocket. I could read it to stave off the boredom on the bus on my way home. A couple of boys with crewcuts presumably on their way home from school passed me on the white country lane. One of them was holding a twig with an insect on it.

'What kind of insect is it?' he asked.

His friend replied, 'Don't you know? It's an inchworm.'

'Hey, can you read this?' Half jokingly, I handed them about ten of the flyers.

'E-NO-KE-N. . . . Oh, Enoken.'

'That's right. Do you know him then?'

'Ages ago, I got taken to the cinema by my dad. It was great. And Enoken was in it. Now, what was it called again?'

'Anyway, Enoken's coming to Sakuramachi.' I laughed. 'Just wipe your nose and listen to me.'

'What do you think?' said one of the boys, looking at his friend. 'It all depends, doesn't it?'

'I want these posters stuck up on the walls of the schools and village offices.'

My idea went according to plan and in this way I was able to distribute three posters and countless flyers in the area. I tried the same technique in the next village. The boys seemed delighted to help and I was spared considerable hard work. The most difficult was Sakuramachi itself, but by the time I arrived in the town, there were very few posters and flyers left. That incredibly heavy rucksack was now as empty as my stomach.

By the time I returned to Tokyo, it was already dark. I went back to Swan Industrial to return the rucksack, only to find Kim-san sitting there in his customary posture, picking his nose, his feet stretched out on the cold desk.

'Hey, have you *tun* the work?'

'Yes, I finished it.' When speaking to Kim-san, I had problems with my own pronunciation.

'Well *tun*. Well *tun*.' He took out a large leather wallet from a drawer and counted out twenty ten-yen notes. '*Ton't* waste it. But what's up? You *ton't* look well.'

'Really?'

'Yes, you look real *pad*. Problems with the ladies, eh?'

'No. I don't have much luck with women.' I realized there was absolutely nothing to be gained from opening my heart to this foreigner with the page-boy cut, but I had come to feel a strange sense of affinity with Kim-san. Of course I was not entirely without ulterior motives. If I were to get on with him, I might well find myself with part-time jobs in the future. I might even receive a couple more packets of the Occupation force Lucky Strikes.

But Kim-san was totally oblivious of the pathetic machinations of a part-time student employee and a wan smile floated across his cheeks, which were marked by the prominent cheekbones so characteristic of many foreigners.

'What's that? You're *stupit*! *Stupit*! You can easily get hold of young woman. You do want, don't you?'

'Well, I suppose you could say so.'

In the dim light afforded by the naked light bulb, the foreigner continued to regale this Japanese student with a torrent of advice. I was troubled by the spit that he occasionally sent flying in my direction, but his comments were not entirely devoid of value.

In his heavily accented Japanese, Kim-san proceeded to inform me of the importance of first impressions in dealing with women. He told me that those who are timid or naturally reticent tend to put on airs in an attempt to win favour with women, but that this would not make a lasting impression with young women. He argued that the young women of the post-war era were attracted to strong men with a powerful streak of individualism.

'Don't mess about! That's it. You have to go for it from the start!'

'You keep talking about not messing about, but what are you actually suggesting I do?' I may have had no problem understanding the need for going all out to create a powerful first impression. But I wasn't altogether sure how to set about that in practice.

'You're *stupit*! Really *stupit*!' He kept criticizing me, but then suddenly he continued, 'You have to talk. Talk about something she won't forget. Any old rubbish will do. *Anyting*, so long as she won't forget.'

'Any old rubbish? . . . But I can't talk like that with a young woman!'

'What? You're *stupit*! *Stupit*!'

So was he telling me that I should stick at nothing in order to create a powerful first impression? That shyness and timidity on such occasions were not to be condoned? Was he claiming that the determination to live life to the full and the energy that foreigners had brought to the black market and other markets since the war should be adapted to the world of love as well?

If one succeeded in making a powerful first impression, at least one could guarantee that the woman would remember one. For better or for worse, this represented a bridgehead. After that, one just had to keep up the pressure. Phone her up and ask for a date. And from the very first date, you should start telling her you love her. It doesn't matter if she rejects these advances. In that case, just make sure she sees you with your next date. That will definitely have some effect.

'What? You show me lady with no *chealousy*! And as soon as she feels *chealous*, she's *peaten*.'

Listening to him talk, I found myself becoming more and more depressed. In Kim-san's native land, they are equally intense about food. They eat their meat larded with hot red peppers. Even their pickles are plastered with peppers. But such customs were unsuited to the Japanese, who prefer more subtle flavours.

'I'll come back for more on this subject some other time. I'm tired.'

'Sure. Come see me any time you need *chob*.'

It was already dark when I stepped outside the office. As I tried opening the ill-fitting doors. I repeated the question that remained on my mind. 'Kim-san, is Enoken really going to appear on-stage in Sakuramachi?'

Kim-san allowed another thin smile to cross his prominent cheeks, but now for the first time he told me the truth. 'Are you blind? Where does it say Enoken? Doesn't it say Enokeso? E-NO-KE-SO.'

Now that he came to mention it, when I looked at the mimeographed paper in the dim light, the final character was not 'n', but the slightly more rounded character pronounced 'so'.

'Oh, I see. Enokeso. But, Kim-san, won't you be had up for this? It's pretty deceitful.'

Kim-san smiled behind his thick-rimmed spectacles and shook his head. He told me that the local people don't expect to be able to see Enoken performing outside the large cities. In the past, he had had Kasagi Shizuko and Yanagiya Gingorō making appearances. And there had never been any trouble.

Everything he said and did was inspired by the same mentality that made him smother his rice and pickles with red peppers. There was no way I could ever match that.

The following day it was raining. The rain beat down incessantly on the tin roof of our apartment. The raindrops seeped through the cracked glass from all angles. In the afternoon street somebody was playing an old trumpet. But they seemed to run out of breath because the sound of the trumpet soon faded away. Then equally suddenly it started up again. Someone was showing great resilience.

Nagashima was working again today. Thanks to the two hundred yen I had earned delivering those flyers, I was able to spend the entire day lazing around in bed. On days like that when there was nothing better to do, I could have made the effort to go to school, but I just didn't feel like going outside and getting wet. My exhaustion seemed to have penetrated to the core of my being.

I stared at the stains on the ceiling. I enjoyed that. As a child, whenever I had been forced to stay at home with stomachache, I would spend the day gazing at the stains on the ceiling in the unusually quiet house. To my child's eye, the stains resembled clouds, animals, even castles in my dreams.

I was overwhelmed by memories of those days. I drifted off to sleep for a while, woke up and then went back to sleep again. There was no let-up in the plaintive tone of the trumpet as it blended with the sound of the raindrops.

The pocket of my raincoat was bulging. I remembered the old magazine I had picked up in the deserted farmyard the day before. It was the kind of magazine full of information about films and the latest popular hits that you find piled up with torn pages in the waiting area at a barber's. I was greeted by the white teeth and forced smiles of actors and singers gazing out from every page. I wondered how these people actually lived. There was really not such a big difference between fellow human beings. Just as I earned two hundred yen for pasting up posters, so they too perpetuated the loneliness of their lives with their white teeth and smiles. As solitary beings, we all need our idols.

'Wherever you may be, you too can enjoy the company of the friendly duo – Ikebe Ryō-san and Yamaguchi Yoshiko-san.' The words leapt out of the page at me. Beneath this was a picture of a smiling couple, a nervous-looking youth and a large-eyed actress who stood with their arms round each other's shoulders. The final yellow page was the 'Readers' Corner'. There were people from Saga and Nagano Prefectures who were so infatuated with certain stars that they wanted to set up local fan clubs. Such feelings of affection form as easily as bubbles on a rainy day, and, equally easily, they evaporate. Maybe the same was true of love.

In order to relieve my boredom, I read each of these, stifling yawns as I did so.

'I am a great fan of Tsushima Keiko-chan. Every day I look at pictures of Keiko-chan doing ballet. How happy I would be if only I could have a sister like Keiko-chan' (*Hyōgo-ken, Muko-*

gun, Ryōgen-mura, Aza Kashio, Kobayashi Shōtarō).

'I'm just a normal nineteen-year-old girl who loves movies hoping to hear from any fans of Wakayama Setsuko' (*Tokyoto, Setagaya-ku, Kyōdō-machi 808, c/o Shindō, Morita Mitsu*).

With both hands behind my head, once more I gazed vacantly at the stains on the ceiling. A voice within me was arguing that if it was women I was interested in, then it didn't really matter whom I chose. For example, how about one of the frivolous girls who sent postcards to the yellow pages of this old magazine? Why not this girl who said she was waiting for someone to write to her?

In much the same manner as I chewed on a cigarette-stub when trying to stave off hunger at work, I placed on the desk a sheet of paper that I had torn out of my university notebook. I had no idea what kind of girl Morita Mitsu might be, but she would probably receive this letter in a couple of days. If things went according to plan, I might even make her mine.

This is how I got to know that girl. This was my first acquaintance with the girl I would end up discarding like a puppy. You can call it a chance encounter if you like. But which encounters in our lives do not stem from chance? And yet chance plays an even greater part in other events during the course of our lives. Maybe the occasion when you first met the spouse with whom you end up sharing the rest of your life was no more auspicious than the time you happened to share a lunch table in some department store cafeteria. However, it has taken me until today to realize that these are no mere trifles, but keys to understanding the true meaning of life. At that time I had no belief in God, but were such a God to exist, perhaps He would chose such insignificant and routine incidents in our everyday lives to reveal His existence. Nowadays, nobody believes in the concept of the ideal woman, but I still look upon that woman as a saint. . . .

My diary (2)

Given the considerable time that has elapsed, it is hard for me to recall exactly what she was wearing that day when we met for the first time. I am sure that in the case of true love, one never forgets the first date, the first touch, the girl's contented smile. But to me, that girl was no more than a passing fling. To coin a phrase popular among the *yakuza*, she was my 'catch', my 'woman' . . . in short, she was a girl destined to be discarded like an empty cigarette-box caught up in the rush of cold night air that envelops a station platform after the last train of the day has just passed through.

And yet, for all the vagueness of my recollection, it is not true to say that nothing sticks in my memory. At her suggestion we had arranged to meet in front of Shimokitazawa Station, which was near her lodgings. (Mitsu had explained in her letter that she would be afraid of getting lost if we were to meet in the more popular Shinjuku or Shibuya, places with which she was less familiar.) I can still recall the overpowering smell of ammonia issuing from the dirty station toilet right beside me and the dirty drops of water that splashed down in front of my battered shoes from the overhead wires that hummed every time a train passed by. It was an all-too-common scene, a Tokyo suburb still struggling to recover from the ravages of war. My heart was racing and I realize now that, in many ways, this was an ideal location for our rendezvous.

Searching the pockets of my grimy raincoat to see how much money I had brought with me, I realized the wisdom of my decision not to arrange to meet in a coffee shop. There was absolutely no need to waste money on a couple of weak coffees, which can cost thirty yen in such places. We students knew of a place where you could get much better value for money a bit further on. I have still not forgotten how, at that moment, the clock in the ticket-office was already showing 5.30, the time we had arranged to meet.

In her letter, Mitsu had explained how she was an office worker in a factory in Kyōdō and that she was not permitted to leave before her work was done. The letter, which ran to ten pages, had been written on cheap paper and placed in a cheap brown envelope. It was written in a careless manner, the characters reminiscent of those of a seven-year-old.

'Are there any fans of Wakayama Setsuko in the university school? On my day off the other week, I saw *The Blue Ridge*, starring Wakayama Setsuko. It was really exciting. I memorized that song and sing it at work. Apart from Setsuko, I also like the new star, Zuruta Kōji.'

She had talked about a 'university school', had written the phrase 'day off' using the wrong Chinese character and – and this was the one that really made Nagashima and me burst out laughing – she had mispronounced Tsuruta Kōji as Zuruta Kōji.

'You've picked a fine one here!' Nagashima's disdain was hardly unexpected. 'Are you going to play the tortoise?'

The notion of playing the tortoise was a popular slang expression amongst students of the time. It played on the image of the woman as the hare about to be caught by the tortoise.

'So what if I am?' I retorted. 'You're a fine one to talk!' But as I stood there engulfed in the smell emanating from the station toilets, I was reminded of Nagashima's comment and was suddenly overwhelmed by a sense of disgust with myself for having gone to such lengths merely to start up a relationship with a young girl.

It was way past half-past five. The people spewing forth from the exit appeared weighed down as they dispersed in every direction. But there was no sign of anyone who answered to my image of Morita Mitsu. An advertising van stopped on the other side of the level crossing and a young man switched on a well-worn recording of a popular song. The speaker was pointing in my direction. I eventually determined to wait for one more train and, if there were still no sign of Mitsu, to call it a day.

'You've been too indulgent.' I ridiculed myself. 'It serves you right. A student like you should. . . .'

Just then I noticed two young girls crossing the lines and looking all around them. They stopped and asked the man in the advertising van something. As soon as he pointed in my direction, I realized that this was Morita Mitsu. One of the girls was walking a few steps behind the other and I was unsure which of the two was Mitsu. As they drew close to me, they both looked thoroughly embarrassed and grabbed each other's hand.

'Go on. You ask.' The short, plump girl with the three shoulder-length plaits whispered to her friend.

'No. You ask!'

I examined their clothes and shoes while I was waiting. Both of them were wearing brownish sweaters and black skirts like those for sale in any market outside suburban stations. The unsightly wrinkles in their stockings suggested they must have been trying to support them with rubber bands above the knee. They were the kind of girls you could spot in any Tokyo suburb. The kind of girls who are often found working in billiard halls or pachinko parlours. The kind of girls who go off to discount movies on Sundays and who take such care of their filthy programmes on the way home. I've really fallen, I thought to myself. I've really fallen. In that case, I thought, I should make the best of a bad job. I determined simply to choose the less unattractive of the two.

'Are you Morita Mitsu?'

The girls just nodded with a frightened expression. My attention was drawn not to the girl with plaits but to her friend who had more prominent facial features.

'Which of you is Morita Mitsu? You?'

My luck was out. Mitsu was the one who looked like a country girl, the one with the three plaits like a primary-school girl.

'What's up? Why have you come together?'

'She asked me to come with her. I told you, didn't I?' The other girl sounded somewhat angry as she whispered to Mitsu. 'I said I didn't want to come.'

I had been prepared all along, not for a formal meeting with a society lady, but for a clandestine date with the kind of woman Nagashima had dismissed as a 'country bumpkin'. But as soon as I was left alone with Morita Mitsu, I was assailed by an overwhelming sense of self-pity. It was a feeling akin to the mixture of disillusion and misery one experiences when discovering that one's name is not on the list of candidates who have passed an examination – even though one never expected to pass in the first place.

'Mitchan. You don't mind if I go home, do you?' There was a hint of respect in her eyes as the other girl looked at me and took her leave of Mitsu.

'Hey, Yotchan. You can't do that!' Mitsu grabbed at her friend's sweater with a look of genuine panic, but the other girl brushed her hand aside and hurried away up the station staircase.

Just at that moment the overhead wires hummed from a passing train and a scrap of paper thrown up by the train wrapped itself around Mitsu's short legs. Looking at her crumpled brown stockings, I was overcome by an acute sense of weariness.

'Help! What am I meant to do, now Yotchan's gone home?' She kicked the ground in front of her as she spoke.

'What's the problem? Haven't you ever met up with a boy before?'

'What do you...? And... I've...'

'Do you go to the cinema on your own on your days off?'

'No. With Yotchan.' At this, Mitsu laughed for the first time. Her smile betrayed a perfect mixture of folly and compassionate concern for others. 'I spend my days off with Yotchan.'

Unable to put up with the smell from the toilet for ever, I moved off. Mitsu followed like a quiet puppy.

'Where are you going?'

'I'm not messing about. I'm going to a place that will surprise you.' This comment was inspired by a sudden recollection of what Kim-san had told me that night. ('You're *stupit*! Really *stupit*! Just give them any old rubbish. Anything will do!') I was suddenly reminded of the miserable figure I must have cut as I eagerly awaited the arrival of this foolish-looking girl. But, having said that, I couldn't simply discard her.

By the time we had reached Shibuya Station it was already dark. A throng of sullen-looking people hurrying home after a long day's work jostled for position on the stairway leading from the platform. In the midst of this congestion, Mitsu was desperately trying not to lose sight of me. She had to scamper along frantically in order to keep pace with my long strides.

'You've got sweat on the end of your nose....'

Hachiko Square was chilly in the late autumn evening air, but there were beads of perspiration on Mitsu's snub nose. The square was packed with men and women stamping their feet.

'I've hardly ever been in such a crowd. Have you?'

'Yes, I have. I used to sell lottery tickets here. If I don't work part-time, I can't go to college.' I was speaking less politely now, partly because she was no lady, but also because there was absolutely no need to flatter this young girl.

'Do you work, then?' Mitsu asked, also adopting a more familiar tone.

'Yes. But it's really tough having to make enough to cover my tuition fees and living expenses.'

I can still remember how at this point Mitsu stopped still and looked at me with a pitiful gaze. She then cautiously put her small hands into the pockets of her cheap jacket.

'What's the matter?'

'You paid for my train-fare, didn't you? I'll pay for myself.'

'Don't be stupid.'

'But if you start throwing your money around... won't you regret it later?'

The lights at the pedestrian crossing at Dōgenzaka turned green and a crowd of people pushed past us into a street lined with cinemas. The two of us were shoved apart by the throng but we were soon reunited. Mitsu continued speaking in a loud voice, totally oblivious of the crowd around us.

'You mustn't throw your money away. I'll pay my own way. That's how it is when Yotchan and I go out together.'

'How much have you got on you at the moment?'

'Four hundred yen.'

Four hundred yen! That was twice as much as I had! I put my frozen hand into my pocket and, as I fingered a crumpled ten-yen note, was overcome with self-pity. I had added the hundred yen I had borrowed from Nagashima to my own hundred yen. That money was precious to me. I couldn't bear the thought of using it all up today.

'Hey, you're quite rich for a girl, aren't you!' An obsequious tone had crept into my voice. 'How much do you get paid a month?'

Mitsu began to talk with pride. It was then that I learnt how her monthly salary as a clerk in the pharmaceutical company in Kyōdō came to three thousand yen, but that, because it was an urban company, she could supplement this by helping out with odd jobs such as packaging. I also discovered that she was sharing an apartment with Yotchan.

'Where do you come from?'

'Kawagoe. Do you know it?'

'No, I don't. Do you go home much?'

Mitsu frowned and shook her head. I got the impression that there were some difficult family circumstances.

It is no longer quite so flourishing, but there was a bar with music that was very popular among us students at the time. Seen in the broad light of day, it was a shabby building that resembled a barn, but by night it looked just like a mountain cottage. It was an untempered wooden building covered in fake ivy with a few lights hanging from the bare ceiling. In the candlelight, the shadows of the assembled youngsters were clearly etched on to the walls. A man in a dubious-looking Russian-style jacket was busy distributing drinks, but occasionally took time out to sing Russian folk-songs to the accompaniment of an accordion placed on his knee. Everyone used to gather in this bar, The Underworld, when in Shibuya – and in The Pits when in Shinjuku.

It seemed as if Mitsu had never been to a place like this and she held back, tugging at my raincoat like a coal merchant on his first visit to the palace.

'Isn't it expensive?'

'Yes,' I joked. 'But you've got four hundred yen, haven't you?'

'Will that be enough? Don't forget my train-fare home.'

I didn't tell her that, far from four hundred yen not being enough, there would be plenty of change from a hundred.

'Are they all students at the university school?' She glanced cautiously around, her attention particularly drawn to a young man in a black sweater who was moving about the room and to a group of young girls wearing berets who were chain-smoking. They were just the kind of Liberal Arts students and girls interested in the theatre whom I found so detestable. They were the sort of people who were fond of describing themselves with sophisticated terms like 'Existentialism' and 'Nihilism', whereas in reality they were just a group of people wearing dirty underwear and foul-smelling socks.

'These are students, just like you, aren't they?'

'Don't be stupid.'

There was something rather affected about the young man who was sitting on the wooden staircase leading up to the second floor playing the accordion. The entire room was enveloped in a purple haze of cigarette-smoke and here and there young men and women began to sing along with the music. The expressions on their faces appeared designed to convey their conviction that singing together was the prerogative of youth, that this was the epitome of cultured living. Something about their blank stares was reminiscent of a chill wind passing by.

'Don't you know this one? . . . It's called "Run, Troika".'

'I don't know it.' Mitsu shook her head forlornly. 'After all, I left school at fifteen.'

'Right! Why don't you ask that man with the accordion to play something you like? How about "The Blue Ridge"?'

Mitsu gazed at the floor in response to my taunts. She had become very restless.

'What's up?'

'Where's the toilet?'

'The toilet? Oh, you mean the WC?'

'Yes.' Mitsu sighed as she removed a packet of tissues from the pocket of her sweater. The place where we had met had been close to the lavatory, but now, as soon as we had sat down, she wanted to go off to the toilet!

We're a foul-smelling bunch, aren't we? I thought to myself.

After Mitsu had gone, I lit a cigarette. Suddenly, however, I was aware of someone tapping my shoulder and I turned around. A young man who had deliberately coated his cap with vaseline and pomade to make it glisten was standing behind me.

It was Itokawa, one of my fellow-students. A pale youth in rimless spectacles, he was the sort of person who keeps snapping his fingers as he walks.

'It suits you.'

'What does?'

Itokawa extended his little finger. 'Girl-friend, eh?'

'You must be joking! Who'd go out with a girl like that?' I said, shrugging my shoulders.

'Never mind! You're only in it for one thing, I bet.' Itokawa sniffed as he spoke. 'In which case, give her one of the cocktails they make here. That's the best and most effective way.'

This bar sold a drink that constituted a small bottle of cider topped up with what was called a 'cocktail' for eighty yen. That sounds very grand, but in effect it was a combination of Japanese *shōchū* and cider. It tasted surprisingly good and so poor innocent girls were liable to knock them back in one. Men just waited for the *shōchū* to dull the girls' senses and to strip them of their powers of resistance.

'Let me order some for you.' Itokawa winked and clicked his fingers at the waiter.

When Mitsu returned from the toilet the waiter had poured a clear liquid drink into two cheap-looking glasses and brought them over to our table. In retrospect, I should have told her not to drink it. But I was painfully aware of Itokawa's gaze focused on us from the opposite corner of the room. If I failed to do anything in this situation, Itokawa would no doubt announce to all my friends that I couldn't even make it with a 'country bumpkin'. At the same time, I was aware of the little voice whispering from somewhere deep within me: 'We're not talking of true love anyway... so why not? Why not?'

'What's this?' Mitsu's good-natured smile returned and I watched as she drained her glass as though knocking back a cup of tea. 'I've never drunk foreign wine like this before. Is it expensive?'

'Hmm,' I replied, a note of fatigue creeping into my voice. 'Well, yes. It's expensive. But... don't worry.'

Her face as she blushed was not attractive and her mouth hung open carelessly.

'This is fun. I should have brought Yotchan. She would have been surprised.' By now, Mitsu was speaking in an even more familiar manner. From his seat in the corner, Itokawa winked at me and that slightly conceited-looking man started playing his accordion again. An elderly gentleman with a wispy moustache and a beret was wandering around from table to table, his back bent with age.

'I wonder if he'd play "The Blue Ridge"?'

'Stop it!' The old man had come up to our table and was whispering something in Mitsu's ear. 'Stop it!' I shouted angrily. 'Don't let him read your palm.'

'It's OK. Here you are,' she said, proffering her hand to the old man. 'I'll pay.'

The old palmist was doing the rounds of the bars and clubs of Shibuya and I'm sure the fortune he predicted for Mitsu merely represented the first thoughts that came into his head. But there was just one comment that happened to come true. He forecast that Mitsu would bring about her own downfall as a result of excessive consideration for others. 'This young girl is far too friendly. She has to be very careful. If not, she'll end up being used by one man after another.' I sneered at this ridiculous assessment and Mitsu for her part started laughing out loud like an idiot. But there was something else the old man said. 'In a few years time, you're going to come up against something you never imagined.' The old man didn't elaborate on this 'something you never imagined' and, greedily snatching up the twenty yen Mitsu had taken from her red purse, he disappeared with a smile.

Mitsu stumbled as she stood up from her chair. Her mouth hung open vacantly and she clung to my arm as she climbed slowly down the staircase, step by step. On the staircase I passed Itokawa.

'Good luck.'

'Are you joking?'

But I had already decided where to take Mitsu next. I remembered from the days when I used to do odd jobs in the area that if you turned left down Dōgenzaka and then climbed up the dark slope that ran alongside the depot for the subway train, there was a Japanese-style inn offering a room for a hundred yen per couple.

The shops in Dōgenzaka were just closing. A shopkeeper, his hair matted with pomade, was standing in the street whistling as he struggled with some duralumin rain-shutters. In a dark corner of the street a middle-aged woman in an apron was trying to sell a whole series of second-hand books and magazines she had laid out on a sheet of newspaper. The covers of the magazines were adorned with pictures of naked women, some with arms bent, others with their head in their hands. Three or four men were leafing through the pages of these magazines with a twinkle in their eyes. A sandwich man with a placard advertising a *coffee shop for couples* smiled at us and mumbled something in a tone of derision. Next, a van selling hot potatoes came squeaking down our winding road and turned into Dōgenzaka.

(Enokeso, eh?) For some unknown reason, I suddenly found

myself wistfully recalling my days spent distributing flyers for Kim-san. Those ink-stained posters with 'Enoken' subtly changed into 'Enokeso'. I may have laughed at the time, but there was no denying that I was the one who had gone round delivering them in those country farming communities that autumn. Just as we had attempted to substitute the fictitious 'Enokeso' for the real 'Enoken', so now I was on the point of deceiving this young girl with the language of a lover. I was aware that, in the past, people had been untroubled by the distinction between reality and spurious imitations. But now, as we looked down on the forlorn lights of Shibuya from the road leading up to Owada-chō that ran alongside the siding by the subway depot, I was forced to reconsider.

'I love you.' I stared at one of the dark street lights at the top of the slope as I spoke, my voice sounding almost as though I were trying to memorize an equation. We were nearly at the small inn with several small windows surrounded by a flimsy bamboo fence.

'Where are we? Is this the station?'

It appeared that my comment had not registered with Mitsu. She just stopped half-way up the dark hill with a look of concern on her face. Puffs of breath could be seen emerging from her mouth.

'Is this Shibuya Station?'

'No, just one more place and then we'll go.'

'If I don't get back soon, I'll be in trouble with my landlady.'

'It's OK. It's still quite early.'

'Er ... you paid at the last place, didn't you? Let me pay half. After all ...'

'After all, what?'

'If you spend too much you'll have problems tomorrow, won't you?' As before, she had put her hands into the pockets of her jacket and seemed to be groping for her purse in the dark. She then quietly held out a grubby hundred-yen note in front of me.

'Stop it.'

'It's OK. I've got some more. And I can just do a bit more overtime. I can get about five hundred yen for five days helping to pack up the medicines.'

For some reason, her voice reminded me of my mother. That was it. That was just how my mother spoke. When I was at junior high school there were serious food shortages due to the war, but my mother had always added some of her own food to my lunch-box. And every time I tried to stop her, she would talk in exactly the same tone that was now being adopted by Morita Mitsu in an attempt to reassure me. She never realized that this had the opposite effect of making her less popular in the eyes of us, her children.

For all this, I placed Mitsu's creased hundred-yen note into my raincoat pocket without a word. 'What's the harm?' I muttered in attempt to eradicate my pangs of conscience.

A station worker carrying a blue lamp crossed the tracks in the siding and disappeared into the darkness. The voice of a drunk shouting in the bar at the bottom of the hill was borne to us on the wind.

'How can you live when you're always thinking of tomorrow?'

The road at Owada-chō that was lined with inns was deathly silent. This was a place where the drinkers from Dōgenzaka would repair with their women. But it must have been slightly too early for that and the place was deserted. I rolled up the hundred-yen note I had just received from Mitsu in my palm and decided to use it to pay for a room in an inn for a couple of hours.

'Let's go in.'

In the small space between the small gate and the entrance some bamboo grass had been planted and a series of stones laid. Both had been thrown together in a somewhat perfunctory manner. The glass door was half-open and inside we could see a range of shoes scattered about. They were arranged in groups, each consisting of a pair of men's shoes and a pair of women's high heels.

'What?' Mitsu looked up at me in surprise and retreated a couple of paces.

'It's OK.' I grabbed Mitsu's arm and pulled her towards me. 'I love you.'

'No, I'm frightened. Really frightened.'

'I love you. Honestly. That's why I took you to that bar, too. That's why I've been walking with you.'

'No. I'm frightened!'

I tried to embrace her. But Mitsu resisted me with a surprising show of strength. Her hair brushed against my face and her body, which reminded me of a rubber ball, wriggled about in my hands.

A volley of random remarks poured forth from my mouth. They were not so much my remarks; rather they were the words that all men formulate as their passion bubbles up like methane gas. 'What's up? What's wrong with two people who have come to like each other sharing a room together? I want you because I love you. There's nothing to be frightened about. I won't do anything to frighten you. Don't you trust me? In which case, why did you come to meet me today? Do you hate me that much? Are you really so repulsed at the thought of my embracing you?' In other words, I resorted to the kind of language that all men use when they are trying to secure a woman they don't love.

'What's the matter? Don't you love me?'

'Yes, I do. I do love you too.'

'See! In that case, show me. We college students need more than mere talk. It was Marx who said that love that isn't absolute is pure egoism.' Of course, that was all nonsense. If Marx had heard that, he would have wept. 'To start with, worrying too much about chastity is old-fashioned. The girls at college are only too eager to put that behind them. It's because they cling to these boring traditions that Japanese women never get anywhere. Didn't you learn all that at junior high school?'

'No. We didn't learn complicated things like that.'

'Right. They don't teach such refined ideas at junior high school. But at university, because men and women are equal, they keep on telling us that, provided there is love, we should throw off this outdated view of purity. You see?'

Mitsu shook her head like a fool. It seemed as if not even one word of my diatribe had penetrated her thick skin.

'What I mean is... you shouldn't create such a fuss in a place like this. We should both go in together willingly. I know it's a bit frightening at first. But, as Hegel said, all progress entails fear.'

What did I care what Marx and Hegel thought! What was the point of all that learning imparted to us by a bored professor in a packed classroom? Surely, if I couldn't make use of it on such occasions, it was just a waste of my time working hard in order to pay those steep tuition fees.

In other words, I felt that this kind of wanton and irresponsible attempt at persuasion was justified. I was convinced that this young factory girl would be overwhelmed by this claptrap from Marx and Hegel.

'Right. Let's go.'

I took Mitsu's hand. But Mitsu pulled her hand back like a child and said, 'Let's go home. Come on, let's go home.'

'Go home?' There was no denying the anger I was beginning to feel towards this girl. She had led me on this far, but now, however much I tried to explain, she was acting like a stupid and stubborn donkey.

'Right. I've got it. I'll go home on my own.' I set off at a brisk pace down the dark hill. I was overcome by a sense both of having missed out and of self-pity at having been unable to have my own way even with a girl like this, and I was furious with her. But it was not just Mitsu. I was equally mad with myself and with Marx and Hegel, both of whom had proved quite useless.

At that moment I felt a pain running from my right shoulder down my back, as though I had been stabbed with a gimlet. I sensed a mild attack of neuralgia in my rib-cage, a vestige of the polio I had suffered as a child. On occasions like this when I was suffering from exhaustion, I would sometimes feel this pain running from my shoulder-blade down my back if I put too much pressure on my arms.

I cried out in distress. But then I set off down the hill again in spite of the pain. I was vaguely aware of Mitsu chasing after me, but I kept on walking without looking round.

She was breathing heavily as she drew level with me and the sound of her footsteps reminded me of a goose. 'Are you mad with me?'

'Of course.'

'Won't you see me again?' she asked forlornly. 'Never?'

'Can't be helped, can it? After all, you've just given me proof that you don't love me.'

'How do you mean, "proof"?'

'Just that! Don't you even know what that means? Since you've absolutely no feelings for me, what's the point in our meeting again?'

'I do like you. I do like you, but I don't want to go to a place like that.'

'In that case, goodbye!'

We had come to the end of the hill and could see the lights from the inns on the road leading to Dōgenzaka and the station. Inside a Chinese food stall a couple of men, their faces red from drinking *sake*, were busy scooping noodles from their plates with chopsticks.

'Won't you meet me again?'

'No.' But as I said this, I was struck by that same searing pain between my back and shoulders. It was even more intense than before. I let out an involuntary cry and moved my left hand to my right shoulder.

'What's the matter?' Mitsu stared at me in surprise.

'It hurts. It's because I had polio as a child. My right shoulder's not straight and I've got a slight limp. That's why none of the girls want to be friends with me. I'm a cripple and so I've never once been loved by a girl.... And now I've been jilted by you too.'

'You've got a limp?' At that moment Mitsu's face was caught in the light from the stall and shone out through the darkness. She was staring at me with a look of sadness in her eyes. She had clearly accepted my exaggerated account at face value.

'That's right. A limp. I've got a limp and so none of the girls go for me.'

'Poor thing.' She suddenly placed my hand between hers, just like an elder sister. 'Poor old you.'

'It's OK. I don't need your sympathy.'

'Have you often been to places like that?'

'How can I? I'm just a cripple none of the girls like. And so today, because I thought you liked me... I thought... right... let's try it out.' I felt no hesitation in using the kind of language you expect from a cheap gangster in a cheap movie. My words were not carefully chosen. I was just motivated by this deceitful instinct. But now for the first time my lies struck a chord in Mitsu's heart.

'Is that right?... In that case... take me there... to the place we've just seen.'

My diary (3)

'Is that right? ... In that case ... take me there.'

We could hear the dull squeak of a train pulling into the siding way up at the top of the hill. At the roadside stall, the two men with their bowls of noodles had turned to stare at us with an air of suspicion.

I can still recall the expression on Mitsu's face at that moment. She was breathing heavily, pausing after every word as she stared sadly at me.... The frightened expression of a child about to receive an injection.... That's it. That was her expression at that moment.

Strangely enough, my feelings of lust had long since dissipated. Instead, for some reason her overwhelming concern evoked in me feelings of compassion and remorse that were totally out of character. I'm the lowest of the low. If I were to take advantage of her kindness for my own gratification now, that would place me beneath contempt.

'A bit late to be talking like that now!' But I maintained my façade. 'Do you really think we can still go there?'

'Are you still angry? Sorry.'

'No, I'm not angry. Just shut up. I don't want to go there any more.' I set off briskly down the alley lined with bars towards Shibuya Station. A drunk bumped into Mitsu, who was following like a puppy, and shouted out, 'Idiot! Watch where you're going!'

'Hey! I can't stand it!'

'What's up?'

'You're marching along like a soldier on parade.'

By the time we reached the main road in front of the station, I had calmed down slightly. When I turned round, there was sweat pouring from Mitsu's snub nose, she was short of breath and had turned somewhat pale.

'Something wrong with your heart?'

'No, I always sweat. Don't worry.'

'Hmm.'

'Sorry I can't make you feel any better... I'm really sorry.'

The dark evening wind whistled down between the shops which were now closed for the day in Dōgenzaka. A couple of groups of bar girls could be seen hurrying down the hill towards the station, holding up the hems of their kimonos with their hands. Some scraps of waste paper were being tossed about in the wind behind them. If I had only stopped to consider why they were in such a hurry to get home, I should have been able to understand why Mitsu was standing so dejectedly in front of me. I had yet to comprehend that these women from Shibuya, too, had their men, their babies, their loves – and that was why they were hurrying through the bitter wind holding their kimono hems up high. And Mitsu...

'What do you want me to do?'

Although it was nearly eleven o'clock, there were still two or three dimly lit roadside stalls in front of the station, and beside them stood a despondent-looking old man from the Salvation Army dressed in a dirty navy-blue uniform and holding a donation-box in both hands.

'Stop it!' He's not selling anything. He's trying to screw you into giving something. He calls it a donation, but then he'll keep your money.'

Suddenly, Mitsu took out her red purse and slipped a ten-yen note into the box. The old man betrayed no emotion as he took a black object the size of a thumb out of the pocket of his uniform and gave it to Mitsu.

'Wow! Look what he's given me!' Mitsu must have been trying to cheer me up. Resting on her palm as she turned to face me was a small, slim crucifix made from molten tin. I call it a crucifix, but it was a ridiculous object that certainly wasn't worth ten yen.

40

'Can you give me three more, please?' Mitsu put three more notes into the box and the old man drew three more identical objects out of his pocket. His total lack of reaction reminded me of a doll.

'What are you going to do with such ridiculous objects? Those are what those "Amen believers" carry around with them.'

'Well, you see... I did have a Buddhist good luck charm. But I lost it.... Here you are. I'll give you one.'

'I don't want it.'

'Take it anyway. If you take this, I'm sure something good will happen.'

The metal crucifix reminded me of those caramels that are sometimes handed out as prizes in the lottery, but Mitsu forced me to accept one and laughed. Her jaw hung open like an idiot's.

'Just go home.'

'Are you sure you're not mad? Will you meet me again? Can I come round to your place when I have a day off?'

My look of anger was intended to show her that on no account was she to do that. I could just imagine how Nagashima and the other students would laugh at me if a girl like this turned up at my apartment. I told her that I would be in touch with her if we were to meet and pushed her off in the direction of the station. She had become a distinct burden to me.

Mitsu kept looking round like a child as she climbed the staircase for the Teito line. After she left, I was immediately overcome by a wave of fatigue. Rubbing my palsied arm, I put my hand in my pocket in search of my cigarettes and touched something small and hard. It was that ridiculous object Mitsu had just given me. I threw it into the ditch in a gesture of defiance. The blackened metal cross fell into the dirty water that was clogged up with scraps of paper and empty cigarette packets.

I returned exhausted to my apartment in Ochanomizu and found Nagashima slouched across the *futon*, his mouth still covered with his mask.

'How was it?'

'What does it matter to you?' Taking off my jacket and trousers, I crawled between the thin sheets that were still imbued with body odour. I had the impression that Nagashima wanted to ask me something else, but I buried my head in the frozen bedding that had never been exposed to the sun and closed my eyes.

That was our first rendezvous. An uneventful and not particularly interesting rendezvous. On the following Sunday, I succeeded in making her mine.

Two days later in the afternoon, I went back to Swan Industrial to ask Kim-san for more work. I was under the distinct impression that he had come to trust me – even to feel some affection for me – as a result of my earlier job with him.

The afternoon sun shone weakly through the ill-fitting glass door. Kim-san was sitting with his feet sprawled across the dusty desk, his finger, as always, inserted into his nostril.

'Ah-ha. You again, is it?' He looked at me with that slightly furtive smile of his. 'You still *ton't* look very *cood*. Jilted by a woman, eh?'

Recalling Morita Mitsu, I smiled wryly. 'I've come about more work. I'm not interested in women.'

'Work... work... work, is it?' Taking hold of a stick of gum, he removed the silver paper and threw it skilfully into his mouth. 'Well, I suppose I can find you something.'

'I'll do anything. I could do some driving or something.'

'This one's a bit *tifferent*. But I'll pay you for it.'

Since this was the man who had unashamedly made arrangements to have not Enoken but Enokeso play in Sakuramachi, I hadn't been expecting anything too conventional from the outset. But when he himself talked about a slightly *tifferent* type of job, that was a signal to be prepared for anything. I remembered an article I had recently seen in the newspaper describing how a gang of foreigners were secretly smuggling goods into the country from Hong Kong.

'You do *motesaseya*, OK?'

'*Motesaseya*? You mean someone who moves things from one

place to another? I'm no good at dangerous work or anything that involves carrying too much.'

'You're *stupit*, aren't you? Real *stupit*!' Kim-san smiled as he blew on to the desk piled high with dust. He then picked up the telephone, dialled a number and started speaking. He was speaking his native language and so I had no idea what he was saying.

'Right. That's OK.' He replaced the receiver and, spitting his gum out on to the floor, he continued, 'OK, student. Are you game?'

The hill at Kudan glistened in the autumn afternoon sunshine and ginkgo nuts rained down on the pavements like golden coins. Some junior high school girls carrying their satchels in both hands were coming noisily down the hill, but on seeing Kim-san with his page-boy haircut and gaudy trousers, they quickly lowered their voices and cast furtive glances in our direction.

'If you don't like *motesaseya*, I give you *tifferent chob*.'

'What's that?'

'You need strong body.' Kim-san suddenly stopped and looked me up and down. 'No. You're no good for that *chob*.'

'Is it physical work?'

'Yes. You work with American ladies. American ladies need man.'

There is no way I could write down what Kim-san proceeded to tell me in a whisper. In short, this other job involved working with nurses from the Occupation forces and other Western women who were all living in hotels in Kanda.

'These women need man. A real man.'

As he continued about their need for a 'real man', Kim-san scrutinized the physical attributes of this pitiful student who lived on cheap fish and stew. It was as if he were evaluating an ox. He then continued with a disappointed expression.

'No, it's no good. You better do *chob* as *motesaseya*.'

I was the one being subjected to such intense scrutiny and so I was more in need of sympathy than Kim-san. However low my standards may have dropped as a student in search of part-time work, still he had no right to start assigning me this kind of task.

Perhaps I look like that kind of a person to him, I thought to myself.

Judging from Kim-san's explanation, a *motesaseya* was not exactly a reputable occupation. He told me there were countless 'weak-willed old men' (to borrow his expression) who lacked the courage to make their own approaches to women. It was the job of the *motesaseya* to assist these old men by helping them to win the approval of the women employees in the bars. In return, the *motesaseya* could expect financial recompense. It sounds ridiculous to us in today's world, but in Tokyo immediately after the war there was a whole series of trades being plied that defy all attempts at rationalization on common-sense grounds. At night in Ueno Park, there were strange men dressed up in women's kimonos and there were men called *kakiya* wandering amongst them looking for clients. *Kakiya* – that is something else which I can't bring myself to write about and I would suggest my readers either ask someone who was around in those times or use their imaginations. At any rate, to us today it was a laughably confused business. But that afternoon as I climbed up from the moat at Kudan to the old officer training ground with Kim-san, I learnt that these trades were no mere figments of the imagination.

Until the war, this had been the location of the Imperial Guard Division. But the place had long since been abandoned to the elements. The dirty water in the moat was littered with rubbish and pieces of wood, and the blackish soil of the training ground was being thrown into the air by the wind in small spirals. Tokyo was still scarred by such derelict areas. This was the era that saw the birth of such incomprehensible businesses as the *kakiya* and the *motesaseya* and in which a chill wind penetrated the lives of ordinary people.

'Where are we going?'

'Over there. You see that man?' Kim-san pointed at a wooden hut that stood on the edge of the training ground. It looked like a stable. A man in a black leather jacket was standing dejectedly beside an old Datsun in the direction Kim-san was indicating.

'This is the student come for the *chob*. He's worked for me before, so he can be trusted.' Kim-san tapped the man on the shoulder as though cajoling him. The man had a scar on his cheek and fixed his gaze on me.

'Can you drive?'

'Yes.'

'Good.' Fortunately I had learnt to drive heavy vehicles at the American base at Machida. 'In which case, you can drive this thing, right?'

'Er ... I think so.'

'Good. Right, if you say we can trust this student....' The man in the black jacket explained that he would leave the car there until the evening. He would leave a suit in the car and I was to change into that and wait outside the strip theatre, Tōtoza, at ten o'clock. There would be a man in his fifties with a skimpy moustache standing there. That was Kameda-san, my client. He had been chief clerk at a certain company for years and had fallen for one of the girls at the Tōtoza. My job was to act as though he were director of some major company when the girl was around.

'So, who am I supposed to be?'

'Haven't you got it yet? You're a *motesaseya*. You have to pretend that your client's a director by acting the part of his chauffeur. I want it done properly. OK?'

'Yes.'

'When you've finished, you must return the car and the suit here tomorrow morning. This time it's three hundred yen, but I'll give you a bonus next time.'

I took my leave of Kim-san and the man in the black jacket and went off down the hill beside the Kudan moat. I spat into the moat and recalled the kind of comments Nagashima and I tended to make as we stared at the ceiling: 'I want some money. I want a woman.' So it was not just poor students like us! Maybe I too would grow up into the kind of fifty-year-old who would hire a *motesaseya* and fall hopelessly for a young dancing girl. But I was being paid for this, so I was in no position to start bemoaning my lot or criticizing the conduct of others.

Just before ten I removed the car from the training ground as instructed, parked behind Isetan department store and walked to the Tōtoza. This was one of those theatres that had begun to advertise strip shows immediately after the war. A man in his fifties with a thin moustache was stamping his feet as he waited at the agreed place. There was something pitiful about him as he looked cautiously around, pretending to read the paper.

'Are you Kameda-san?'

'Yes,' he replied, wiping his nose with his hand. 'You must be the *motesaseya*.'

'That's right.'

'I'm relying on you,' he whispered rather diffidently.

He removed his handkerchief from his pocket and blew his nose. He was the kind of upright, rather shy man who would have commuted from his house in the suburbs to his job for years without missing a day's work. I could almost see him on Sundays, lying around listening to the amateur singers on the radio, scolding his children and then, in the evening, enjoying a bottle of second-rate *sake*. Then one day, this upright, rather diffident man had been taken to one of these shows as a joke by a younger man in the company and had fallen for a dancer there.

But what would a dancer want with a fifty-year-old man with a wife and children? He must have dreamt of what might have been were he a company president or director. Every day at work, he must have stared jealously from the sidelines at the figure of the director, a man of about his age but with more impressive credentials.

I was suddenly overcome by a fear that a similar destiny lay in store for me. The thought of carrying on with such a dreary existence was more than I could bear.

'Shall I summon her?'

'Yes, please.'

'What's her name?'

'Um.... She's called "Grape" Inada.'

There was no one on the staircase at the Tōtoza, but I could hear the sound of a trumpet from somewhere up above. A young man in a yellow sweater sat studying a musical score in front of a door marked *No entry*.

'Can I see Grape-san, please?'

'What do you want? No, you can't.'

But the five Lucky Strikes I had received from Kim-san soon brought a knowing smile to the face of this man, who reminded me of a sand eel.

'Grape-chan. There's a client for you.'

Several naked forms were moving around behind the door. Some of the girls were standing by a table eating *ramen*. Others wearing gaudy dresses were milling around smoking. One of the girls emerged from the crowd and walked towards the door, scratching her behind.

'What do you want?'

'The director's ...'

'The director?'

'Yes, Kameda-san, the executive director, is waiting downstairs. Apparently he wants to treat you to dinner.'

'Eh?' The girl stopped scratching herself and opened her eyes wide. She was wearing false eyelashes and eye-shadow. 'Is that old man a director?'

All of a sudden, her stupid face reminded me of Morita Mitsu's face when she smiled. Mitsu and this girl would have been born and raised in very similar circumstances.

'Just a moment. Please wait downstairs. What? You mean, that man's a director?'

'He's my boss.'

I closed one eye and laughed and then ran down the staircase. Kameda-san was stamping his feet and leaning against the wall of the theatre. He looked cold.

'Well, was it OK?'

'Yes, please cheer up. Remember, you're an executive director.'

By the time I had brought the car round from the back of

Isetan and sat my timid friend with the moustache down in the passenger seat, the girl was standing there wearing a loose-fitting green coat. Or perhaps, rather than a coat, it would be better described as one of those cloths they place over billiard-tables.

The girl was chewing gum and humming something through her nose. 'Wow, I'm starving!' she protested.

'Where shall we go, sir?' I asked as I started the engine.

But Kameda-san just gave vent to a plaintive cry as though suffering from constipation. It was my job in such circumstances to arrange everything.

'The restaurants in Shinbashi and Tsukiji are rather too conspicuous, don't you think, sir? And, in my opinion, those places are not quite suited to a secret rendezvous, sir.'

'Um.'

'Would it not be preferable to entertain this girl in the Shinjuku district?'

Next, turning to the girl who was sitting as though in a daze, I remarked, 'When you become managing director, life's nothing but meetings. He rarely shows his face in places like Shinjuku.'

'I had no idea he was a director.'

'That's right. He's always stressing the importance of modesty and economy to us employees. And he always practises what he preaches.'

'Are you Kameda-san's chauffeur?'

'Yes, and I also serve as his secretary.'

Strangely enough, the more I kept up this façade as I drove, the more I came to feel as though it were true. But glancing in the rear-view mirror, I could see the uneasy look of concern on the face of Kameda-san sitting edgily on the back seat, his fingers pressed against his dirty collar. He was in need of a drink to build up his confidence.

I stopped the car in front of the Mushashino-kan. Between here and the station lay a whole series of tiny bars huddled together like matchboxes. The whole street was saturated with the smell of oil, of fried chicken, and of clams and other shellfish being cooked, and there were women everywhere, each vying for custom for her own establishment.

'This is a nice popular place, sir. Why don't you take a short walk with the lady?'

As Kameda-san left the car, I nudged his shoulder and he reeled backwards. Come on, pull yourself together! Otherwise it's undignified and the young lady won't fall for you, I thought to myself. But Kameda-san just asked, 'What can we have around here that isn't too expensive?'

'What do you mean? You only need about a hundred and fifty yen and you can drink more than enough.'

While waiting for them to re-emerge, I went up to one of the stalls and tucked into some well-broiled whale-meat.

Back in the car, I was growing tired of waiting when the girl came running up to me, her coat flapping in the wind, and said. 'It's no good! That boss of yours ... he's drunk.'

'Oh no!'

But now was the time for me to fulfil my obligation as a *motesaseya*.

'Just a minute. There's something I need to tell you. Our director, Kameda-san, is crazy about you. Really crazy. Please be kind to him tonight.'

'What do you mean, be kind to him?'

'Just what I said. Don't you understand?'

All of a sudden, this girl with the false eyelashes and eyeshadow burst into peals of laughter. 'You still don't understand, do you?'

'Don't understand what?'

'You're really stupid, aren't you? Didn't Kim-san tell you?'

Kim-san? Kim-san? What was all this about Kim-san? But then opening her mouth wide and laughing in a most unseemly manner, she told me the most extraordinary tale.

It transpired that this girl, too, was part of the deal arranged by Kim-san and the man in the leather jacket. Clients like Kameda-san remain in blissful ignorance as, with the help of the *motesaseya*, they convince themselves that they have won the girl's heart. In that way, it is better for the girl involved and easier to fleece the client of his money since, having in-dulged himself with the woman, the client ends up paying both the girl and the *motesaseya*. In this way, the woman could squeeze him for money and Kim-san and the other man could claim their own commission as well. This was twice as effec-tive as the technique used by a simple go-between.

'Oh, I see,' I remarked with a wry smile. 'That's what it's all about, is it?'

Kim-san was full of schemes like the 'Enokeso' saga. Every-thing this foreigner did was carefully thought out. There was a hidden dimension to all his plans.

Kameda-san was in high spirits as he returned to the car, his moustache still showing traces of *sake*. He was chewing a toothpick and mumbling, 'I love you. I love you.'

Looking at me out of the corner of her eye with a crafty smile, the girl said, 'Don't you think we should find a place where this gentleman can lie down and recover from his excesses?'

Realizing that this was a good way to hurry matters along, I asked Kameda-san if he agreed.

'Yes, let's do that.' In stark contrast to his earlier manner, Kameda-san was by now in fine fettle. 'Driver. Take me to that place. If you don't hurry, you'll be out of a job.'

As I drove, I found myself once more wondering about Kameda-san's life-style. The small house in the suburbs to which he returned after a full week in the office. The children's un-derwear hanging up to dry on the veranda. Kameda-san on Sundays crouching down in his white long johns in the gar-den making the dust-box his wife had requested. Next, I pic-tured him lying back listening to the amateur singing contest on his battered old radio. Then, from the following day, it was back for another week of uninterrupted work.

The street lined with Japanese-style inns in Sendagaya was eerily quiet. The headlights of our old Datsun picked up the mice scampering about behind the grey fences and piles of rubbish. As though fully aware of the situation, the dancing girl had pressed her face to the window and was singing.

'That girl I left behind that day.
I wonder where she's living now.
I wonder what she's doing now.
There's no way of knowing.
But, from time to time, my heart throbs.
As I recall the girl I left behind that day.'

'What's that song?'
'Don't you know it? It's one of Dick Minee's oldies.'
'Really?'
Kameda-san and the girl were deep in conversation on the back seat. Ten minutes later, the two of them passed through the dimly lit entrance of the inn.

Mitsu and I passed through the dimly lit entrance of the inn and pushed open the glass door without a sound. A row of unpolished men's shoes and women's shoes with battered heels was lined up on the concrete slab at the entrance.

A maid with a somewhat stiff expression emerged into the hallway asking whether we wanted a short stay or the whole night. Somewhat tentatively we both followed her up the staircase, aware of the stale smell that emanated from the toilet. We could hear the squeaking sound of the toilet door being opened somewhere at the back of the building.

After the maid left, Mitsu and I sat down in front of the pot of cold tea and a small dish. Mitsu sat stiffly with both hands on her knees staring at the ground. Meanwhile, trying to conceal my embarrassment with a yawn, I set about reading the message on the paper wrapper for the bean-filled wafer on the dish.

'The taste of these wafers designed for two.... So that was it, was it?'

The wall was dotted with fingerprints and smears of dark blood from squashed mosquitoes. To prevent people peering in from outside, wooden slats had been affixed to the small window. In the corner of the room there was a thin *futon* and a grimy white water-jug.

Outside, a steady drizzle was falling. Looking out between the slats, I could see a woman carrying an umbrella climbing wearily up the slope that Mitsu and I had walked down in the midst of our heated discussion one week earlier. In the rain-drenched railway siding, a solitary train was being shunted into the depot by a man dressed in oilskins.

'Right. . . . Shall we lie down, then?' I tried to speak as cheerfully as possible, but my voice was hoarse and sounded hollow. 'Come on. Come over here quickly!'

But Mitsu just sat there rigidly staring at the wall.

'Come on. I'm lonely.'

Was I really lonely? Not a bit of it. I knew only too well at what stage Mitsu would surrender. There was just one prediction made by that palmist in that dirty Shibuya bar that was accurate. 'You are far too friendly.'

It was not so much that Mitsu was friendly. Rather she had this habit of empathizing with anyone who appeared wretched or bitter. And this was more than just empathy. Forgetting herself completely, she would do her utmost to comfort the person in need. She must have acquired this ridiculous sensitivity over the years from the sentimental movies and the amusement magazines such as *Bright Star* that she looked at on her days off.

That was exactly how she was with me. In spite of her adamant refusal to enter this inn, all I had to do was to mention my childhood polio, admittedly with a certain degree of exaggeration, and all her resistance melted away like snow. Inspired by cheap compassion and cheap sympathy, she clasped my hand between hers and started to whisper something to me. And so, on our second date, I had been able to take advantage of her delicate sensibility and bring her here with no hint of resistance.

'I'm lonely. Won't you come and cheer me up?' Burying my head in a pillow, I laughed inaudibly. Look at that! It's worked like a dream! But you're bad. Evil! A really evil fellow! But I'm not the only one to lead a woman on like this. Look at Kim-san and the man in the leather jacket. And isn't this just the same as Kameda-san with his thin moustache. This is how everyone else behaves, so I'd be crazy not to go ahead now.

I pulled Mitsu down towards me and, as I did so, she hid her head in her hands. It was then that I noticed a dark spot about the size of a coin near her wrist. It was like a slightly swollen boil. It stood out as a weird and unseemly dark patch on her white arm.

'What's this?'

'Oh, nothing. I've had it for about six months now.'

'Have you had it looked at by a doctor?'

'No. It doesn't hurt or itch.'

All was silent for a while. Then Mitsu whispered, 'Don't look. I'm shy.'

'What's there to be shy about? And what's this? You're still wearing this, are you?' My hand touched the good-luck charm she had purchased the other day. For want of a proper chain, she had hung the crucifix around her neck with a piece of thread that looked like a shoelace.

'Get rid of that!' With a violent tug I ripped the thread and flung the cross down on to the *tatami* mat.

It was all over within seconds. The whole experience was a disappointment. A real disappointment. All of a sudden, the *tatami* mats scorched by the sun, the walls with the finger-prints and splotches of blood where mosquitoes had been crushed, the *futon* and the water-jug – all things that had been of no concern to me earlier – now struck me as dirty, even sickly. Even Mitsu, who was still lying face up on the bed like a corpse, looked bedraggled and unappealing. The two or three hairs plastered to her cheeks which were streaming with sweat. That unsightly flat nose. That brownish sweater. The dark spot I had seen on her wrist. Her man's vest. I had slept with this drab-looking girl! My lips had kissed her drab-looking body!

The cigarette tasted unpleasantly bitter. The drizzle was still falling against the slats on the windows. The sky was over-cast, clogged with clouds the colour of old cotton. And the dreary yellow streets of Shibuya stretched out below. Today, too, Kim-san would no doubt be sitting in his office with his legs stretched out on his desk. Kameda-san would no doubt have walked the muddy streets to his office holding his umbrella against the rain. 'I hate it! I hate it! I hate this life!'

'You know . . .'

'What?'

'Was that your first time?'

'Shut up!'

'Have you stopped feeling lonely?'

I sat down on the *tatami* mats and put on my socks and jacket. It was somehow an effort to talk to Mitsu. If at all possible, I should have liked to slip out of the inn on my own and breathe in the rain and fresh air.

I don't want to sleep with her ever again. Once is enough.

Some thirty minutes later, I left Mitsu at Shibuya Station. She seemed to be trying to cheer me up and followed me like a puppy all the way to the platform for the train for Yoyogi where I was to change. But I maintained a stubborn silence. I had no particular reason for disliking this girl, but the thought of spending even one second with this 'country bumpkin' after our moment of passion was more than I could bear.

A voice came over the loudspeaker urging all passengers to stand behind the white line and, before long, a crowded train glided into the platform. I was standing right in front of the doors as they opened.

I boarded the train without saying a word, without even looking round at Mitsu.

'Please. . . .' Behind me I could hear Mitsu shouting something. 'When can we meet . . .?'

But the doors shut before she had time to finish her sentence. Who would want to meet up again with a girl like you? You're a total stranger to me now. You're as much a stranger as the people with whom I happen to rub shoulders or who happen to tread on my toes on this train.

As the train slipped slowly out of the platform, I experienced a cruel sensation of joy and turned to face the doors.

Mitsu was running along the platform, her mouth open in surprise and one hand slightly raised. She was chasing after the train, trying not to lose sight of me.

But soon the image of her looking dejectedly in this direction, her face covered by the three plaits of hair and her snub nose, receded far into the distance.

The train shook noisily. As I listened, I found myself recalling the song the dancing girl had sung in the car, her face squashed against the window.

'That girl I left behind that day.
I wonder where she's living now.
I wonder what she's doing now.
There's no way of knowing.'

The spot on the wrist (1)

The clock in the packaging-room struck seven times and there was a stifled yawn. Yotchan – Yokoyama Yoshiko – tapped her mouth several times with the palm of her hand, stretched and said, 'I'm shattered. I'm going to stop.'

It was called the packaging-room, but in reality it was no more than a cold room of about a hundred and fifty square feet, with wooden panels lining the walls. Yotchan threw a bottle of ointment into a box and picked up the kettle that sat on the brazier.

'Are you going to carry on?'

Morita Mitsu accepted the cup of boiling water her friend had poured for her and answered in the affirmative.

'You've been so calculating just recently. What's up? All you're interested in is your overtime money.'

'Leave me alone.'

'But if we leave it much later, the water in the bath-house will be all dirty. And this morning Taguchi-san was making all sorts of nasty comments again...'

'What?'

'Yes, I was amazed. Didn't you hear? You went home last night without shutting the door, didn't you?' Hanging her smock stained with medicine on the wall, Yotchan began to massage her right shoulder. 'So, just leave it. I'm going home.'

'Feel free.'

'OK. Goodbye.'

'Goodbye.'

After Yotchan had left, the factory and the corridors were even quieter. As she continued with her work, Mitsu listened to the wind that occasionally whistled through the darkness. The wind hummed through the electricity wires and rustled the leaves of the trees in the grove that lay opposite the factory. This may have been part of greater Tokyo, but one could still find various types of oak trees here in Kyōdō.

The express trains on the Odakyū line out of Shinjuku stopped first at Shimokitazawa and then here, but it still took twenty minutes. Other areas of the Setagaya ward of Tokyo such as Daita, Umegaoka and Gōtokuji had all been ravaged in the air raids in the spring of 1945 and the fires had spread right to the outskirts of Kyōdō. But luckily they had been quenched in the vicinity of Kamimachi. As a result, even now after the war, one could still see in between the houses the thatched farmhouses and the groves that stood as constant reminders of the former Musashino district.

Outside the station there was a small shopping arcade. Here, one could still find greengrocers selling the bamboo shoots that were grown in the area in spring and the local barber who had been head of the Kyōdō division of the army reservists during the war. Then there was Matsubara, the electrician's which had been started by a local landholder as a side interest. At the end of the arcade lay a still undeveloped area given over to onion fields. The soap and medicine factory at which Mitsu was employed stood right in the middle of this undeveloped area.

The factory was no more than a two-storey, square building made of wood, erected on the site where, after the war, a couple called Wakabayashi had begun producing home-made soap. Theirs was an incredibly smelly soap made from fish oil which failed to produce any real lather. But this was an era when one could sell absolutely anything and the Waka-bayashis were soon in a position to employ a few people and to expand the business. At this point, their attention was drawn to a certain type of home-brewed medicine that was effective against the skin disease erysipelas that was prominent in the region, and so they turned their hands to medicine as well as soap.

There were four male employees working with Yotchan and

Mitsu. In addition to office work and running errands, the girls helped with the packaging. They would clean the cans containing medicine oil with benzine and then place them in boxes. On the night-shift they also packed soap.

This was the fifth time Mitsu had worked overtime. Until now, when work finished at five, unless specifically requested to stay on, she would eat the meagre meal of rice and boiled fish provided by the factory and return to her apartment as quickly as possible. She would then go to the public baths and, on the way back, she would take a leisurely stroll with Yotchan through the arcade or stand reading comics in the lending library. But since 'that day' her whole attitude had suddenly changed. She had become cold and calculating.

'Another five times and I'll have made a thousand yen.' The night-shift rate was a hundred yen. This was her fifth night of overtime, so her pay-packet on the twentieth of the month would include an extra five hundred yen.

As she thought of that thousand yen, Mitsu broke into an involuntary smile. Shortly after meeting the student from the university (for that was how she described Yoshioka to Yotchan), Mitsu had happened to notice a yellow cardigan in the Saegusa, the clothes shop in the arcade. Unlike the unattractive sweaters you see in the station forecourt markets along with various coats and jumpers, this was a cardigan like the ones worn by the actresses Takamine Hideko and Sugi Yōko in photos in *Bright Star*. So soft it felt as though it would melt when touched, it looked as light as a feather. Until now, Mitsu would always have dismissed such a sweater as an unaffordable luxury. But now she was overcome with a burning desire to buy it. And then there were the men's socks. She must buy those, too. After all, he had been wearing his torn socks with the heels reversed. That evening as he had removed his socks, he had scratched his feet in embarrassment as he told her, 'When the heel's gone, we wear our socks back to front. The holes are covered by our shoes, so nobody can see them.'

She tried to imagine how happy he would be when she gave him three pairs of socks at their next meeting. As she wrapped another piece of soap, Mitsu found herself laughing out loud. 'I'll go to his apartment and do his washing for him. I'll take a needle and thread and then I can fix some of his socks.' She pictured herself standing at his sink in the full glare of the sun washing his shirts and underwear. She could vaguely recall a scene in the movie she had seen about three months earlier in which a young girl was tackling a pile of washing for her student lover. All this to enable him to spend the day studying! Ever since the incident in the inn, Mitsu had been overwhelmed by a longing to do his washing.

I too can be of some help. I want to be just like that girl in the movie.

'What are you up to?' Suddenly, there was a sharp tap on the window of the workroom. It was Taguchi-san, a middle-aged employee who served as factory watchman by living in the compound with his family. He always laid heavily into Yotchan and Mitsu. 'You're not allowed to stay after eight. We can't have you breaking the rules.'

'But . . .'

'No "buts" about it! You went home last night, too, without shutting the door, didn't you? Just imagine if something disappeared. I'm the one who'd take the blame.'

Taguchi-san was inclined to pontificate at length. He just went on and on saying the same thing over and over again as though seeking to remove a piece of gum caught in his teeth. As she listened to the sound of the wind outside, Mitsu whispered to herself, 'So what? I hate Taguchi-san!'

When she arrived home, Mitsu was grateful that Yotchan had remembered to leave the kitchen door unlocked. The two of them were renting a second-floor room from a *shakuhachi*[1] teacher called Shindō-san. It was a four and a half mat room in the middle of the second floor that had formerly been used for storage and virtually no sunlight penetrated that far even on days when the sun was shining.

Yotchan was lying on her bed nibbling salted beans and

1. A bamboo flute

looking at a movie magazine. She was a fan of Ishihama Akira and had stuck several of his photos on the wall. On one occasion, she had sat there sucking her pencil and written him a letter. Mitsu could still remember what she had written: 'Ishihama-san, how are you? I am fine and working hard, so please don't worry. I have seen all of your movies. I am working in a factory in Kyōdō. I. . . .'

That was all perfectly true. Not only had she seen all his movies, she had gone to Shimokitazawa to see some of them two or three times. Yotchan had posted the letter in the box opposite the factory and then every day had waited for his reply. But he had not replied.

'Did you lock up properly?' said Yotchan, looking up from her magazine.

'Yes. I was told off by Taguchi-san again.'

'I hate him. He's a really nasty piece of work.'

The two girls nourished a deep-rooted animosity towards Taguchi-san. In the first place, he was particularly unpleasant to the two of them. But it was not just that. He also delighted in discussing their physical attributes with the other male employees in a deliberately audible manner. Such comments were invariably accompanied by his particularly obnoxious laugh.

But the real reason the two girls hated Taguchi-san was as a result of an incident that had occurred some years previously. A young female clerk called Miura Mariko had worked in the company for a couple of months. One day when Mariko was in the factory toilet, there was a sudden flash of light from the opening used for sewage. Next, a silver object the shape of a rice tub was pushed into the hole. It was a bucket. Someone had placed a bucket over his head and was peering up from the hole. Mariko shrieked and ran out of the toilet, but the man with the perverted sense of humour had already fled. However, it had not taken much for Mariko, Yotchan and Mitsu to identify the guilty party.

In the old days, Mitsu would probably have teamed up with Yotchan and begun reviling Taguchi-san. But now, as Mitsu listened to Yotchan speaking ill of that middle-aged employee while she nibbled her salted beans, her thoughts were elsewhere. A persistent rain had fallen from the clouds the colour of old cotton wool and, from the window of that inn, she had looked out on the damp slope and the streets of Shibuya. The plump young girl struggling up the hill. The misery and the terror of that evening. If only it had been possible to do so without incurring Yoshioka's wrath, she would never have gone ahead. But Yoshioka had argued that that was required as proof of her love for him. Faced with such an argument, Mitsu had been completely at a loss. She had eventually acquiesced on the grounds that she would thereby be sparing Yoshioka a degree of sadness. For some reason, ever since childhood Mitsu had been unable to endure the sight of someone looking sad. And such feelings were accentuated when such sadness was on her account. That is how it had been that evening. The time spent in that inn at the top of the hill that rainy day represented a few minutes of wretched endurance.

Mitsu was too naïve to be concerned about pregnancy, but she found herself unable to confide in Yotchan. This was the first secret that had existed between the two girls to date, but now she maintained an embarrassed silence about everything that had taken place. . . .

'I'm going to sleep.'

'Right.'

Mitsu resolved to think about something different. Something more pleasant. As she lay there in the darkness, she pictured that yellow cardigan in the 'Saegusa' in front of the station. If only she were wearing that, she could go anywhere with Yoshioka without succumbing to that same sense of nervous diffidence.

Two weeks had passed, but still there was no word from him. Every day as Mitsu returned from the factory, her heart pounded at the thought of the postcard or letter that might be waiting for her at home. She tried to look as casual as possible so as not to arouse Yotchan's suspicions but, even at work, the thought preyed constantly on her mind. After work as she returned to Shindō-san's apartment, her pace involuntarily quickened in the hope of finding that letter waiting for her. Sometimes, she even broke into a run. Breathlessly, she would open the glass door at the back and glance at the step at the foot of the stairs on which Shindō-san always placed their letters. But for two weeks there had been nothing. The faint glow of evening sunlight was concentrated on the second and third steps of the staircase, accentuating the specks of dust in the air.

It's bound to come tomorrow. She clutched the good-luck charm that hung round her neck and tried to convince herself. I'm sure it will come tomorrow.... It's bound to.

But the following day, too, she clutched the charm and uttered exactly the same prayer.

She had bought her previous good-luck charm at the temple in Kawagoe. But that was now lost. Mitsu had been born and bred in the town of Kawagoe in Saitama Prefecture. A large old town, established as a post station with a commercial base, it had escaped the fire bombing during the war and as one walked the streets one could still see the fire tower and the remains of the castle and the old houses built in the traditional storehouse style. But Mitsu had no plans to return to this old town, her home town, for she knew only too well that relations between her father and stepmother were better when she was physically absent. Mitsu was the only child born to her father by his first wife who had subsequently died, and his second wife had brought three children of her own. The new wife was not a bad woman, but, even as a child, Mitsu had been aware that her existence represented an obstacle to her mother-in-law's happiness. Mitsu was unable to live with the knowledge that her presence was the source of misery for another and she felt unbearably sad when confronted by the unhappiness of a fellow human being. It was for this reason that she had moved to Tokyo and found a job like this.

Sunday came. Every Sunday, Mitsu and Yotchan went to the Nanpuza behind the Kyōdō shopping arcade after lunch. The Nanpuza was the only cinema in town, showing two movies for forty yen. The cheap programme that left blue ink-stains on the hands. The babies crying in the pitch-dark cinema. The old men smoking away quite casually and the acrid smell emanating from the toilets. But the two girls were quite content to gaze at the silver screen, licking the dried cuttlefish they had bought at the stall. Even before watching, they had a vague idea of the plot of the movie from *Bright Star*. Yet to both of them there was a world of difference between knowing the plot and actually living the scene.

However, this Sunday, instead of going to the Nanpuza, the two girls took the train from Kyōdō to Seijō. They had been making plans for this trip for several days now.

Seijō was home to several of the stars of the silver screen. The home addresses of the stars had been listed at the back of one of the magazines and, as she sat there studying these the other evening, Yotchan had commented: 'Wow! Tazaki Jun lives in Seijō, too. And so does Tsukioka Chiaki.'

The fact that, to the best of their knowledge, at least seven famous actors, including Mifune Toshirō and Fujita Susumu, lived in Seijō, must have been due to the area's proximity to the well-known T Studio. On realizing this, Yotchan had asked Mitsu to accompany her to Seijō the following Sunday. She wanted to see with her own eyes the homes of the stars of whom she dreamt.

Seijō was only eight minutes from Kyōdō on the Odakyū line. As the two girls timidly left the station forecourt, they were confronted by a road lined with cherry trees that stretched out before them in a manner reminiscent of the exclusive Tokyo suburb of Den'en Chōfu. A row of Western-style houses surrounded by cypress trees lent the scene a foreign air and, at that moment, a young foreign boy emerged on his bicycle from a gateway that opened out on to a beautiful lawn. He was whistling to himself.

'Heh . . .'

'Wow.' Yotchan and Mitsu looked at each other and sighed in disbelief. It was so different from the residential area in their own Kyōdō. So this was there Tsukioka Chiaki and Mifune Toshirō lived. The girls were overcome by the realization that they were breathing the same air as these stars.

The two girls continued down the road like proud cockerels with bright red cockscombs. The road was lined with houses with name-plates on which were inscribed foreign names such as *James* and *Dan*, and from inside one of these, they could hear a large sheep-dog barking and could make out the strains of some beautiful music.

They wanted to ask someone where the various stars lived, but everyone they passed seemed to belong to a different class and they lacked the courage to approach them. The afternoon sun reflected off the roofs and windows of the cream-coloured houses and the two girls continued walking with pounding hearts until the sky began to turn pink.

'Look!'

Startled by Yotchan's outburst, Mitsu asked, 'What's the matter? You'll give me a heart attack.'

'Look, this is Deko's house. You know, Takamine Hideko.'

Apart from the roses held in place with wire netting, it was a simple Japanese-style house with none of the flamboyant, modern touches that might be expected of an actress. But the words *Takamine* and *Hirayama* were clearly embossed on the name-plate on the gatepost. As avid readers of *Bright Star*, the two girls were well aware that Hirayama was Takamine's real name.

'So it is!'

'Yes, it really is!' Yotchan was standing bolt upright, her face and body taut with nervous tension. Inside, the house was deadly quiet, suggesting that no one was home. Suddenly, for no apparent reason, Yotchan slipped into the shadow of the gate and began toying with something.

'What are you doing?' Mitsu watched in surprise as Yotchan opened the lid of the milk-box and removed an empty bottle still covered in creamy smears.

'Leave it alone. What if you're caught?'

'What are you talking about? This is what's left of the bottle of milk Deko drank this morning. Don't you want it? I've ... I've just got to take it home as a souvenir.'

Not content with the milk bottle, Yotchan also picked up a pebble that was lying in the drive, claiming that Deko may well have stepped on it.

All the while, Mitsu looked at Yotchan with a series of complex emotions. For some reason that she was unable to identify, during these past two weeks, Yotchan's actions, which until then had never struck her as particularly strange, had suddenly come to seem incredibly childish. Two weeks earlier, just like Yotchan, she too might have been desperate to carry off a pebble from Takamine Hideko's driveway as a memento. But now, somehow or other, such conduct struck her as absurd. Yotchan was still a young girl. A naïve young girl. She was infatuated with Ishihama Akira and Sata Keiji, yet that was the extent of her knowledge of the world. However, Mitsu had now shared an adult secret with Yoshioka-san. The realization induced in Mitsu a wave of sadness and, at the same time, made Yotchan's actions appear incredibly childish.

'Heh,' she said to her friend, who was still foraging around like a hungry wolf. 'Let's go.'

After that, the two girls came across the house of another of their idols. This time it was the home of the comedian Kishikawa Akira. A baby-faced comic actor who had a beautiful voice but was as fat as a sumo wrestler, he had often appeared on stage with Deko. It was just the kind of stylish Western house one would expect from a movie star, and a large *futon*, big enough for two to sleep comfortably, was hanging over the washing-line. Mitsu instinctively recognized that it was designed for a double bed, but Yotchan commented, 'Wow! So Kishikawa sleeps on a *futon* like that, does he? He's twice, even three times as big as we are, so he needs a *futon* that big!'

It was almost evening by the time the two girls arrived back in Kyōdō. The light from the lamps in the arcade was blurred by the damp, greyish mist. A stream of parents exhausted from a Sunday out with the family in Shinjuku and Mukōgaoka Amusement Park stepped off the train holding on tightly to their children.

Mitsu left the station amongst this throng and said, 'Just a minute.'

'Where are you going?'

'It doesn't matter. Just wait here.'

Mitsu left Yotchan and rushed off to the arcade. Under the fluorescent lighting in the show window of the 'Saegusa', she could see the fur-lined jackets and the ski gloves that were already on display. Staring through the glass at the yellow cardigan in the right-hand corner, she was relieved to discover that it had not yet been sold.

Mitsu sighed. It was a light cardigan that felt as soft as fleece. It was up to Mitsu to clock up enough hours of overtime by the next pay-day on the twentieth.

Every month, on the afternoon of the twentieth, the six employees gathered in the main office with their personalized seal. There, either Wakabayashi-san or his wife would hand over the brown pay-packets to each employee in turn.

That morning, Mitsu arrived at work before everyone else and started cleaning the factory. But all morning she was totally preoccupied by the clock on the wall in the packaging-room. The time usually flew by, and before Mitsu had had the chance to stop and think, it was time to set out the dishes for the chairman and for Funada-san, Yamauchi-san and Onuki-san, the three employees who did not bring their own packed lunches. Today, however, the time dragged interminably.

As Mitsu prepared lunch, the chairman's wife said to her, 'What's up, Mitsu? Why do you keep going to the packaging-room?'

But since this was pay-day, the six employees were all in good spirits. Even the young male employees, who on other days were apt to assail Yotchan and Mitsu with coarse remarks, went about their work singing popular songs.

After lunch, the chairman set off for the bank on his bicycle wearing a light jacket, and when he returned a short while later, sweat was streaming down his cheeks.

'Right. Let's see if I can pay you well today!'

Everyone stopped work and collected their seals from their coats that were hanging from hooks on the wall. One by one, in descending order of age and length of service, they entered the office and received their brown pay-packets from the chairman. Young female employees like Yotchan and Mitsu came right at the end.

'Happiness always comes last.' Yotchan smiled at Mitsu. 'That's what my mother always used to say.'

When Mitsu and Yotchan entered the small office, the afternoon sunlight was streaming in through the windows. The chairman sat opposite Taguchi-san and was shaking his head.

'It's no good. This is a small town factory and I've always looked on everyone as part of the family. But this is the fourth time you've asked for an advance.'

'Yes, I've been trying my best not to borrow. But just this once. . . .' Taguchi-san glanced at Mitsu and Yotchan out of the corner of his eye with a look of displeasure in his eyes.

'Oh, it's you two is it?' The chairman gave the impression of wanting to conclude the matter quickly and, turning to the girls, merely said, 'One for Yokoyama Yoshiko and one for Morita Mitsu.' Thumbing through the pages of the company register, he continued, 'Two overtime shifts for Yokoyama and ten for Morita, is it? I see. . . . Don't waste it.' Taking an envelope from the drawer, he added on their overtime payments.

Taguchi-san spat on the floor and rubbed the spittle with his shoe in silence.

On leaving the office, the two girls rushed back to the packaging-room. They could now indulge in the pleasant secret ritual of pay-day – furtively counting the notes in the envelope.

Yotchan let out a mouse-like squeak and then spoke up. 'That will serve Taguchi-san right, won't it? When he gets an advance, only a tiny bit goes to his family. He spends the rest on cards and drink.'

The card game involved, called *koi-koi*, was a kind of Japanese pelmanism and Mitsu had often seen Taguchi-san engrossed in a game with one of his colleagues during the lunch-break. But nothing could have been further from Mitsu's thoughts at that moment. She recalled the evenings she had spent in the silent packaging factory during the past two weeks, listening to the wind as she rubbed the cans with benzine. With this hard-earned thousand yen she was now in a position to acquire that yellow cardigan. She could also buy the socks for Yoshioka-san.

'Heh, Yotchan...I... I'm just going to slip out for about fifteen minutes.'

'What? What are you going to do?'

'I'm going to buy something.'

'What are you going to get?'

'Something nice.'

Taking off her overalls and slipping on her wooden clogs, Mitsu went outside into a cold wind. The wind was enough to lift particles of dust high into the sky, enveloping the factory like a smoke-screen. The trees in the grove behind were singing. By the gate, Taguchi-san was talking with a woman who was weighed down with a baby on her back and holding another child by the hand. Mitsu caught snatches of their conversation borne to her on the wind.

'No! When I say no, I mean no!' Taguchi-san scuffed the ground with his shoe as he shouted.

'But, please....' The woman was Taguchi-san's wife.

'It's not just my fault. Now, go home.'

Sensing that this was no time to stand there listening, Mitsu hid behind the glass door. After a while, Taguchi-san returned towards the building, his clogs ringing out on the ground.

'She's such a pest. Always asking for things...' Taguchi-san was talking to himself. He then disappeared into the toilet.

Mitsu closed the glass door silently and hurried towards the gate. Mrs Taguchi was still standing in the road, looking dejected. With her baby on her back, she and the boy, who must have been seven or eight, were being battered by the wind.

'Hello.' Mitsu smiled at her.

'Hello... heh, where are you off to?'

'Just to the arcade. I want to... buy something.'

'It's all right for some! I can't even think of shopping at the moment.' Mrs Taguchi was trying to keep the baby happy as she began to grumble. 'I don't know. Here we are on payday, and still....'

Mrs Taguchi explained that she had to pay for three months of school meals for the boy the following day, but even then her husband refused to co-operate. 'He hasn't even bought the school satchel the boy needs. I'm doing some work on the side, and my husband just takes advantage of that. I'm thinking of giving up all my work, but it's not quite so simple.'

Like her husband, Mrs Taguchi tended to pontificate at length. Every time the baby grew fractious, Mrs Taguchi rocked her shoulders. The young boy was staring fixedly at Mitsu, his mouth agape. He had a small spot to one side of his lip.

'Really? That's too bad.' Mitsu laughed in a perfunctory manner before continuing. 'Well, I'll be seeing you.' She cut the conversation off abruptly, bowed hastily and moved off. There was a short cut from the factory to the arcade that ran between two enclosed lots of wasteland. She had to buy that cardigan just as soon as possible.

'Mummy, let's go home. Come on.'

Behind her Mitsu could hear the boy pestering his mother. The baby started to whimper again.

'Come on!'

'Be quiet!'

The wind blew specks of dust into Mitsu's eyes. It coursed through Mitsu's heart. A voice was borne to Mitsu on the wind. The sound of the baby crying. Of the peevish boy. The sound of the mother scolding her child. The Shibuya inn she had visited with Yoshioka-san, the damp *futon*, the woman wearily climbing the hill outside. The rain. The tired face of one gazing down with pity on these lives whispered to Mitsu.

Won't you turn back? That money you've got would really help those children and that mother.

But.... Mitsu tried desperately to resist that voice. But, I worked hard every night. I really worked hard.

I know. The voice replied sadly. I know. I know just how much you want that cardigan and how hard you've worked for it. And that is why I'm asking you. I'm asking you to use that thousand yen for that mother and her children instead of for that sweater.

Why should I? After all, it's Taguchi-san's responsibility.

There's something more important than responsibility. The important thing in this life is to link your sadness to the sadness of others. That is the significance of my cross.

Mitsu could not fully understand the meaning of this last comment. But the image of the small red spot on the side of the mouth of that child who was standing there in the wind tore at her heart. The sight of anyone enduring unhappiness made her sad. Mitsu always experienced a profound sense of sadness when confronted by the sufferings of a fellow human being. Slowly but surely, that red spot was proving more than she could bear.

The wind blew specks of dust into Mitsu's eyes. It coursed through Mitsu's heart. Wiping her eyes, she turned back.

'Mrs Taguchi.'

The mother and her children looked back and gazed at Mitsu in amazement.

'Mrs Taguchi. I'll lend you this.' Mitsu held out the thousand-yen note she had been clutching. The eyes above her snub nose betrayed a tearful smile, but she continued gamely. 'But don't tell Taguchi-san.'

Mitsu was suddenly aware of a pain in her wrist. About half a year ago, she had suddenly developed this coin-sized scab. It was slightly swollen, like a boil. Usually it wasn't painful or itchy. But Mitsu recalled how that night when she had been held by Yoshioka-san, she had experienced a searing pain in her wrist, if only momentarily.

More than two weeks had passed, but still there was no word from Yoshioka-san. Mitsu wondered what had happened to him. Was he sick? If he were sick, he would be lying there with no one to care for him.... Mitsu grew increasingly concerned. She had been told in no uncertain terms that she was not to visit his apartment. But she felt that, if he were sick, she had a duty to go and look after him.

The weather was fine the following Saturday afternoon as she put on her old brownish sweater and left her apartment. When she came to the Saegusa she quickly averted her gaze and hurried past. But the image of that soft cardigan, after which she had hankered for so long yet which she had ultimately been unable to buy, was branded on her memory.

Can't be helped.... It really can't be helped.

Ever since childhood, Mitsu was well versed in resigning herself to something. She was not the sort to oppose her own destiny: rather, she would accept it.

Yoshioka-san had written his address on the back of the envelope that had contained his initial letter and Mitsu had guarded it as a treasure. It was now in the pocket of her sweater, carefully folded. Scrutinizing the map of Tokyo in the office, she had found that she must leave the train at Ochanomizu Station.

She took the Odakyū line to Shinjuku and changed to the JNR line. Twenty minutes later, as she was leaving Ochanomizu Station, she showed the address on the envelope to the young official who collected her ticket.

It was an unusually warm Saturday in early winter and on the hill at Surugadai there was a stream of students wearing college caps and young girls with handbags going in and out of the bookshops and coffee shops that lined the street on both sides. Mitsu stared at those shops and college students, wondering whether Yoshioka-san was amongst them.

Following the instructions given to her by the station official, Mitsu turned left into a side-road at the bottom of the hill, just before the railway lines. On a couple of occasions, she was obliged to ask for further directions, once at a local tobacconist's and once at a small shop selling the kind of leather belts popular amongst students. However, she reached her destination without too much difficulty. The cracked glass on the door had been covered over with thin strips of newspaper, and the door squeaked noisily as she pushed it open. The bright sunlight shone on the entrance piled high with soiled army boots and shoes with broken soles and down the deserted corridor. It was a depressing scene. The place was a mass of empty, dusty apartments.

'Excuse me,' Mitsu called out.

'Who is it?' Mitsu's call was answered by a middle-aged woman with a towel wrapped round her head. The duster she held in one hand suggested she was busy cleaning. She looked up suspiciously and asked, 'What have you come about?'

'Um... well... I've come to visit Yoshioka-san.'

'Yoshioka-san?' The woman looked Mitsu up and down before continuing. 'Are you a friend of Yoshioka-san?'

'Is he here?'

'No. He just vanished without telling anyone where he had gone. He left without paying his last month's rent or his electricity bill and there's a great hole burnt in the *tatami* mat in his room. I don't know what to do.'

'Where did he go?'

'That's just what I want to know. I let him have the room without a deposit and this is what happens. The students these days are not as naïve as they used to be. What a cheek!'

Mitsu ran out of the building without fully understanding what was happening. The sweat trickled down her flat nose as once more she climbed the hill at Surugadai. The road was still packed with students in their carefully polished caps.

'Hey, how about some mah-jong tonight?' One of the students was speaking to his friend.

'No. I want to play billiards.'

Their casual manner of speaking reminded Mitsu of Yoshioka. Stopping in front of one of the bookshops, she wondered whether Yoshioka-san might not be inside. But all to no avail. She also tried looking through the windows of the coffee shops. But of course there was no sign of Yoshioka-san. Dusk was gradually approaching and the sky over Ochanomizu Station had turned pink. The crowds were beginning to gather around the ticket-vending machines. A young man on a bicycle threw a pile of evening papers down in front of a kiosk before pedalling off. As she lingered at the wicket wishing she could meet Yoshioka-san, Mitsu could not bring herself to buy a ticket to Kyōdō and just stood there staring blankly into the distance like a fool. Blankly, like a fool. . . .

All thoughts of Morita Mitsu disappeared without trace from my mind. I was not in the least interested in where she was or what she was doing and rarely found myself thinking back on our two meetings. As of a ship gradually disappearing over the horizon, my mental image of her was reduced to a single line, then to a small dot and was eventually obliterated. I was convinced that she was a total irrelevance in my life and that things would continue in that vein.

And yet – and yet there were just a couple of times when I found myself recalling those two meetings. Like that of a cloud that appears fleetingly over a desolate mountain landscape in winter, her shadow passed in front of my eyes.

It was the spring of the following year. At that time I had a part-time job monitoring advertising balloons. It was not a particularly onerous job. All I had to do was to sit in the sun on the rooftop of a department store and check that the balloons from which the adverts were suspended were not blown away in the wind.

From the rooftop, the city of Tokyo could be seen stretching out in all directions. It was dusk and the sky over the horizon had turned a darkish blue. As I watched, the setting sun resembled a dullish red glass ball as it slowly sank from view. The constant buzz of cars and trains below wafted up to the rooftop as a melancholy sound and I could see people moving about in the windows of the neighbouring buildings. Here and there I could make out rows of houses that appeared no more than matchboxes and, beyond them, the vast city stretched out into the distance, forlorn and indistinct. Out there were countless homes inhabited by countless people, but I was suddenly aware that each of these people was involved in the process of living, just as I was.

So many lives. A whole spectrum of lives. Leaning against the railing that had grown quite cold, I muttered absently to myself. Everyone in this town is experiencing the ups and downs of life together.

It was at that moment that Mitsu's face appeared in my mind's eye. I found myself wondering where she was and what she was doing in this town enveloped in greyish haze and smoke. It reminded me of that popular song.

But that was all. Like garbage that floats to the surface of water before being engulfed once more in the depths, such sentiments, so alien to me anyway, soon disappeared.

There was, however, one other occasion when I remembered her. As I sat waiting my turn at the local barber's, my attention was drawn to the edition of *Bright Star* that was included amongst the old magazines and weekly journals which were strewn about on a chair. The cover was torn, but to pass the time I began to flick through the pages. As I did so, I came across the advice column. Most of the letters were from silly girls seeking advice on their domestic situation, employment possibilities or on their relationships with their boy-friends. But there was one that clearly resembled the situation between Mitsu and myself.

I no longer remember how the letter was composed, but this girl too had made the acquaintance of a student by letter and, despite her 'sacrificing her innocence' after just a couple of meetings, the student had subsequently disappeared from her life.

Of course the letter did not carry the name of Morita Mitsu. In all probability the letter was not written by Mitsu. But since this was a carbon copy of the tenuous relationship that existed between the two of us, it is hardly surprising that I found myself thinking of her.

The columnist was a cultured lady whose reply seemed totally logical. In brief, she recommended that, since this student had forfeited his right to love, the sooner the girl could forget this irresponsible man and embark on a new life, the better.

I looked up from the magazine spread out on my knees. The sleepy rays of the afternoon sun shone down on the barber as he continued with his work. A young boy was toasting some rice cakes dipped in soy sauce on the stove.

An irresponsible man who had forfeited his right to love? I experienced a vague sense of anger and resentment directed at the woman who had concocted that reply. So who do you think you are? With a face like the sole of my foot! Looking down on life from on high with that supercilious air of yours! Mumbling some gratuitous rubbish that was of no use to anyone! Just as the muffin-maker produces a constant stream of muffins, you just keep churning out simplistic and hackneyed advice in response to your readers' concerns. If anyone's being irresponsible, it's you, isn't it?

'Yes sir, that's the way of the world.' The barber was replying to some question from his client. 'We're all the same in that respect.'

I threw the magazine back on the chair. That was the extent of my thoughts about Mitsu. That and no more.

About a year passed. Thanks to Kim-san, there was no shortage of weird jobs when I needed them and eventually I succeeded, even if by a rather roundabout route, in fulfilling the requirements for graduation. It was the time of the onset of the Korean Incident. Of course at that time all of the private universities were experiencing financial difficulties and so there was a steady flow of students entering and leaving the universities. It was for this reason that both Nagashima Shigeo and I were able to stay on the conveyor belt and emerge from the university gates, rolled diploma in hand, and confront the outside world without ever attending classes on a regular basis and with grades that were cause for no pride whatsoever.

'Hey you, goodbye.'
'You, too.'

Nagashima and I shook hands and parted company on the hill at Ochanomizu. It is one thing to share the same ricepot, as the saying goes, but we had even shared the same underwear! We had no idea what to expect in the big wide world, but we were both determined to lack for neither money nor women.

Both Nagashima and I were fortunate in that, thanks to the sudden boom in the economy as a result of the Korean Incident, neither of us experienced any difficulty in securing employment. Needless to say, we could not emulate the graduates of Tokyo University who walked straight into the top banks and trading companies. But then we had not set our sights that high in the first place.

I entered a company in the nail wholesale business in Nihonbashi. There were only about twenty employees excluding the chairman, Shimizu-san, and the directors, Yoshimura-san and Kataoka-san. But presumably, thanks to the monopoly order we had established with one of the top nail-producing companies in Ōtemachi, both the current situation and prospects for the future looked bright. I entrusted my future to this company.

Better to be the head of an ass than the tail of a horse!

Full of pride, I included this proverb that I had learnt as a student in a letter I sent home. I felt as though a ray of light had finally penetrated my life after years of living at the mercy of part-time jobs.

In addition, only a few of the fifteen male employees had been through university. Of the new intake, I was the sole college graduate. As such, from the day I entered the company, I was unable to divest myself of the sense that I was the object of a certain degree of adulation amongst the five female employees.

I must at least become the head of the ass.

I convinced myself that, rather than becoming the tail of a large beast – rather than being content on the lowest rung of a large corporation – it was much better to be the driving force of smaller fry. As I stood in the subway train on the way to the office, I would often picture myself, ten or fifteen years hence and, on such occasions, I would break into an involuntary smile. In contrast to the seats reserved for the regular employees, the directors, Yoshimura-san and Kataoka-san, sat in large revolving chairs and their desks were covered with sheets of well-polished glass. They even had their own telephones. And every morning when they arrived at the office they were greeted by a chorus of 'Good-morning' from the employees, who all stood up and bowed. At that point, a young woman called Hirayama would present them with a cup of tea. That just had to be myself in fifteen years time.

In which case, what's the best way to get there? With this in mind, I bought four or five books with titles such as *The Secret of Success* and *How to Advance Your Career* at a second-hand bookshop. They were all extremely vague and lacking in specifics, but there was one translation of an American work entitled *The Magic of Conviction*. The author of this book claimed that if one repeated one's aspirations in front of a mirror every morning, it would result in a state of self-hypnotism and ultimately endow the individual with an inexplicable power to realize his or her dreams.

I determined that anything, however ridiculous, was worth trying for the sake of securing advancement in life.

Come lunch-time when everyone was out for a stroll and the office was deserted, I would enter the wash-room alone and repeat, 'I will succeed. I'm going to succeed.'

Gazing at my own reflection in the mirror, I mumbled the formula outlined in the book. On such occasions the face I saw reflected in the mirror was like the pathetic image of a man struggling with a prolonged bout of constipation. But, for all that, I was deadly serious.

On that day too, I was standing in front of the mirror in the wash-room. The office was deserted and I was convinced there was nobody around.

'I will succeed. I'm going to succeed.'

As I spoke, I sensed someone standing behind me and, looking in the mirror, I saw the reflection of another face in addition to my own. It was that of a young woman.

'Well!' She was even more taken aback than I was. Her name was Miura Mariko and she had entered the company a year before me. But since she was the niece of the chairman, even the directors tended to address her as 'Madam' out of office hours.

'I thought we had a burglar!'

'There's no peace here, is there?'

'Sorry!' But she laughed in amusement. 'I mean. I come back early from my walk ... and there's this strange hoarse voice coming from the back of the office. I was so frightened, I wondered if I should tell someone.'

She then drank some water from the wash-room cup and, still holding the cup, stared up at me with a look of surprise.

'You're a strange one, aren't you, Yoshioka-san?'

'Why's that?'

'Instead of going out with everybody else, you stand there in the wash-room talking to yourself.'

But at that moment, my mind was elsewhere. Her eyes were beautiful. They were black and sparkled like crystals. Her lips were still moist from the water she had just drunk. I could even see drops of water on her white throat.

For some unknown reason, at that moment, I found myself recalling something Nagashima had told me over a bowl of rather pathetic-looking *zōsui*. It was his story about the female grape-pickers. Listening to him talk, I had been overcome by the urge to meet a woman like this.

That poignant desire welled up alongside another feeling in my mind. Unlike the first urge, this second was of a more utilitarian, rather devious nature. This young woman was related to the chairman. There could be no harm in winning her approval. At the very least, if I could ingratiate myself with her, it would doubtless pay dividends sooner or later.

'It can't be helped. There are so many things we newcomers have to do. Take the abacus, for example. This is the very first time in my life I have handled an abacus. Every night I dream of being chased by an abacus with feet!'

'That's true.' Mariko laughed again. 'You are always walking around with your abacus and sighing. That's one of the things you graduates are hopeless at, isn't it?'

'Hey.' I suddenly assumed a serious air and went on the offensive. 'Will you teach me? You're good at it, aren't you?'

'But . . .'

'But what? You know what Hegel said – those in positions of authority should teach their charges as a duty of love.'

I can still vividly recall the look on her face at that moment. I was greatly taken by her expression as she first gazed at the floor and then, fingering the cup she was holding, she glanced up at me with a look that betrayed both concern and embarrassment. It was in stark contrast to the dumb, if kind-hearted, smile that had been the hallmark of Morita Mitsu.

We used the coffee shop near the office for our lessons. She remained faithful to Hegel's dictum. And I, for my part, remained an enthusiastic student. For a start, it was only natural that a college student unable to use an abacus would become an object of ridicule for those who had finished their education after graduating from junior or senior high school. Equally, however, I was motivated by a desire to win her approval.

'You've got a really logical mind.'

'I told you so.'

'In no time, you're going to be better than me.'

'Oh, come on. Any animal, however lazy, can be taught to perform tricks if it has the right trainer.'

None the less, as far as possible, I avoided outward displays of friendship towards Mariko when we were in the office. It would have done me no good at all if rumours had started flying amongst my peers that I was currying favour with the chairman's niece.

For a young lady, providing personal tuition on the abacus to a new recruit and witnessing his consequent improvement was by no means a negative experience.

'Wow, Yoshioka-san's really taken off recently, hasn't he?' It was Yoshimura-san who sat opposite me who made this remark one day.

'Not at all. I've still got a long way to go.' I glanced over at Mariko as I answered and I could not fail to notice the way she stopped writing and the faint smile, suggesting the joy of victory, that passed across her face at that moment.

I'm in with a chance here. For some reason, that was my immediate reaction.

I found myself interpreting her decision to tell no one of our sessions in the coffee shop (I am tempted to call them 'our secret classes', but that would be a slight exaggeration!) as an act of true friendship. At any rate, when the chairman asked her one day how the new employees were coming along, I knew she would never speak ill of me in such circumstances. Indeed, I was convinced that she would do all in her power to improve the reputation of her own pupil.

You've said the right thing there, I thought.

I remembered Kim-san telling me that the first thing required to win a girl was a pre-emptive strike. According to Kim-san, in order to make a powerful impression on her, it was important to keep up a flow of trite remarks. But I now came to realize that it was possible to avoid such uncouth and pushy language and to resort rather to a more psychological and refined approach.

At any rate, the more I thought about Mariko, the more I found the very existence of Morita Mitsu, with whom I had merely shared one brief fling anyway, receding into the dim and distant past. It was as though she no longer existed at all. And yet I remained totally oblivious to reality. To the fact that all our dealings with others, however trivial, are not just destined to vanish like ice in the sun. I was unaware that, even though we may distance ourselves and banish thoughts of a fellow human being to the recesses of our minds, our actions cannot simply disappear without leaving traces engraved in the depths of our hearts.

Having said that, I do not believe I was any more scheming or crafty than your average man. Aren't there the odd occasions in the life of most men when they act as I did with

Mitsu, even if in a slightly different manner? And isn't every 'salary man' able to empathize with the altruistic desire I betrayed in seeking to ingratiate myself with Mariko in an attempt to win the chairman's approval?

In short, whilst readily acknowledging that I was no paragon of virtue, I was equally convinced that I was not a particularly evil person. I was just one of the numerous 'salary men' living in Tokyo, seeking no more than an uncomplicated and mundane existence devoid of excessive turbulence.

And so. . . .

And so, my desire to draw closer to Miura Mariko was not simply a case of my seeking to use her for the sake of furthering my career. There was no doubt that I had come to like her and I was certainly attracted by the sight of that beautiful mouth glistening after a drink and of the innocent look on her face as she smiled when our eyes met.

Some two months after I joined the firm, there was the company excursion. The trip was organized at the suggestion of the chairman, Shimizu-san, as a means of improving relations between the new employees and the others. Since this was the season when the new leaves would provide a colourful backdrop, it was decided that we should go to Lake Yamanaka, one of the five lakes of Mount Fuji.

It was a Saturday. We travelled to Gotenba by train and then boarded the bus which the company had hired for the purpose. As we crossed the plateau, the brilliant June sun was glistening on the leaves, but the twenty employees were more interested in sharing the sweets they had brought with them and singing all the songs they knew than in admiring the scenery outside. A man called Sayama-san who had joined the company some two years before me was an expert on the harmonica and accompanied our songs.

'Hey! Yoshioka-kun and Mari-chan are getting hot.'

'They sat next to each other on the train and they're at it again on the bus!'

In the face of such comments, Mariko replied, 'Don't be silly! There's nothing between us at all.' Once more, Mariko's smile suggested both concern and enjoyment. But it is quite true that we sat together all the way from Tokyo to Lake Yamanaka. In the office, I was always so careful not to betray my feelings for her. But now that we were away from the company, I appeared to have relaxed my guard. There was no real barb to the comments that were being bandied about and we were not in the least perturbed.

'Where did you work before you came to the company?' There was a note of nonchalance in my voice as I sucked on the caramel she had given me and gazed at the undulating forest on both sides. The leaves on the windswept trees glistened in the June sunshine. 'Out in the country? At your father's place?'

'No.' Her reply was totally unexpected. 'I had a spell doing clerical work at a pharmaceutical factory in Kyōdō. It was only a small firm and I soon left.'

Kyōdō! A pharmaceutical firm! The words rang a bell. When was it? ... Yes, that was it.... The place where Mitsu worked! No ... surely not!

'A pharmaceutical firm?' My voice was suddenly muffled. 'You mean a factory producing medicines?'

'Yes, that's right. It started off making soap, but then they added a pharmaceutical division.'

'Was there a girl working there called Morita ... Morita Mitsu?'

'Yes, there was! She's the girl from out in Kawagoe, right? Do you know her?'

'No ... I don't.' I hurriedly held my tongue. 'My friend was ... well. ...'

Of course she failed to detect the look in my eyes at that time. If she had noticed anything, I would presumably have deflected her suspicion by claiming I was feeling sick because of the sun streaming through the windows.

Before long we were looking down on a bluish-green lake. The lake was ringed with forests of deciduous pines, the red and yellow roofs of villas and lakeside hotels, all strung out like a line of sweets. The young women squealed with excitement and clamoured to be first off the bus.

There was still a month before the summer began in earnest, but already most of the souvenir shops and restaurants were open.

'Can you buy me a film?'

'I think I'll have a drink.'

On the lake we could see a motor boat driven by what appeared to be an impetuous soldier from the Occupation forces. He and his family were in their swimming costumes, enjoying a day out. The boat raced off in a straight line far into the distance, its wake forming a white arrow on the surface of the water.

'I love daring things like that.' Mariko made this casual comment standing by the shore, the waves lapping at her feet. Her headscarf billowed gently in the breeze blowing from the lake. 'Do you do any sports, Yoshioka-san?'

'Um, I can ride.' As a matter of fact, I had never ridden a horse in my life. And I paid the price for my attempt to impress.

'Gosh, you ride?'

'Well yes, a bit.'

'That's wonderful! Can you show me? I'm sure there's a place for hiring horses around here.'

I was aware that she had caught me out. But it was too late. On the opposite bank we could see a group of men who appeared to be local farmers standing around smoking with three or four horses tied up in the shadow of a souvenir shop.

Mariko stood up and set off, leaving me, for my part, thinking, Well, that's done it! But as I followed her, I tried to convince myself that everything would be fine. After all, they were only local pack-horses. They weren't about to run wild. However, I was slightly concerned about my bad arm.

As expected, all the horses were old and doddery. They were thin and bony with mucus clearly visible in their eyes, and they were surrounded by horse-flies.

As the two of us approached the horse-hiring booth, the other employees began to look at us and laugh. Right! I realized that, if everyone was going to watch, I had to put on a good performance.

The farmers smiled as they watched me cling to the horse and raise one leg to the stirrup in a manner that suggested I was grovelling. The horse just blinked disconsolately and wriggled, as though seeking to rid itself of some unwanted burden.

'Is this your first time?' the farmer asked contemptuously.

'Are you joking?' I replied.

'Right! So you don't need any help.'

I had been left with no alternative but to respond in this way in front of Mariko, but this was my first time ever and I was amazed at the size of the horse. I felt as though someone had placed an enormous grey table between my legs.

'Giddy up.' The farmer gently touched the horse's buttocks and the horse set off. From the way it sauntered, I gathered it was quite old. It seemed to be seeking to draw attention to the ridiculous nature of its lot.

'Yoshioka-san. Hang on there!' The girls from the company clapped their hands in encouragement.

'Right, I'll show them.' The men were looking up at me with a tinge of jealousy in their eyes. I laughed as the horse and I passed slowly in front of them.

It was not difficult. I felt relieved. This horse wasn't about to run wild or rear up out of control. I should hold the reins with confidence.

I turned round and smiled at Mariko. Mariko smiled back, her white teeth gleaming. Behind her lay the lake, a glistening silver backdrop. Above us lay the blue sky of June.

Then suddenly the horse stopped, put its head to the ground and refused to move. Not only that; it then began to eat the grass. 'Giddy up! Giddy up!' I shook the reins and tried kicking it gently. But the horse just carried on eating, oblivious of its rider.

'What's up, Yoshioka-kun?'

'Let's see you ride, then!'

I grew angry and began to sweat. At that point in full view

of everyone I struck the horse a resounding blow on its buttocks. The horse was still chomping at the mouth as it eventually set off again, shaking its head. It was clearly out of sorts.

I turned round once more and smiled at Mariko. The lake behind her was still glistening silver, but Mariko was looking at me with a slightly perturbed expression. Above us lay the blue sky of June.

Once more the horse stopped. This time, it was lashing out at the horse-flies with its long tail. The flies began to gather around my own sweaty face.

'What's up? You don't know what you're doing, do you?'

'The horse knows its rider. When it sees a useless rider, it refuses to move and makes fun of them.'

Such comments were clearly intended for my consumption.

Right, damn it! I'll show them I can ride! This time I lashed out at the horse's buttocks. The horse whinnied, stamped its feet and then moved noisily off in the direction of the white road, bathed in sunshine.

Once more I turned round and smiled to reassure Mariko. Mariko stood in front of the glistening silver lake and was looking at me with a tense expression.

The horse stopped. Here we go again, I thought. I heard a dull sound beneath me. The horse was relieving itself! Five seconds. Ten seconds. Still it continued! I was amazed how long it took for the horse to finish its business. The dull noise sounded as if it would continue until Judgement Day.

'Ha ha! I can't watch. Look at his horse!'

'Yes, and it's not just pissing, either!'

It was true. Oblivious to the world, the horse had turned so that its large rump pointed straight at the women in our company, lifted its tail and began its more serious business. An unpleasant smell wafted up from below and I was consumed by a sense of shame, as though I were the one who had committed an indiscretion in public.

Unable to bear any more, I crawled down from the horse. Left once more to its own devices, the stupid horse then proceeded to trot calmly back to the rental booth all on its own in a most calculating manner.

The women in the group averted their eyes in sympathy and sought to stifle their laughter. The men on the other hand began slapping each other on the back and ribbed me mercilessly.

By this stage, Mariko was nowhere to be seen. She must have been incapable of looking me straight in the eye.

None the less this failure by no means worked to my disadvantage. Not only did the incident serve to reduce the distance that had previously existed between myself, a college graduate, and my colleagues, but Mariko for her part seemed intent on assuaging my dejection with what came across as a show of maternal love. During lunch and throughout the ensuing bus journey she stood up for me and stared at me with a look of sympathy in her eyes.

That evening, we boarded the bus once more and set off on the return journey. To avoid returning by the same route, it had been decided we should make a slight detour and return via the Gotenba highway.

As dusk arrived, the sun shone luxuriously on the fields and forests and on to the various hamlets we passed through. Mount Fuji revealed itself to us in all its splendour, a spectacular purple form.

'I'm sorry.' Mariko leant towards me as she spoke.

'What for?'

'For making you ride that horse.'

'Don't be silly. No problem! As they say, even monkeys fall from trees.' I was feeling perfectly content. Those student days living as a tramp. The *zōsui* and cheap fish we used to eat. Those part-time jobs I was given by Kim-san. Delivering the 'Enokeso' posters. That was all in the past. Here I was, an ambitious young man determined to make it to the very top.

I wondered how Nagashima was doing. I was determined to succeed in life. Quite determined.

Under the evening clouds I caught sight of a row of wooden barrack-like buildings in the middle of a grove. Strangely enough, there was not one farmhouse in the vicinity. Those buildings stood there all alone. I wondered whether they were the remains of some military installation, but this impression was belied by the presence of some foreign-looking buildings in the compound.

'What's that? A school?' One of our number, Ono-san, had also noticed the buildings and addressed his question to the bus girl.

'Which one?'

'That one, all alone over there, that looks like a barracks.'

'Oh, I see,' the girl nodded. 'That's the leprosarium.'

'A leprosarium?' Ono sounded surprised. 'Leprosy? You mean God's way of punishing wrongdoers?'

'That's right.'

'Help! Shut the windows! We mustn't let the germs in!'

Everyone laughed. But several of our group did proceed to shut their windows nervously.

The leprosarium had been constructed in an isolated area in the middle of the woods. Presumably, owing to fear of infection, there were no farms or houses in sight. Under the lingering grey clouds, the fields and buildings huddled together in melancholy silence, the dark shadows seeming to exude an indescribable sense of sadness.

'They should send all lepers to some remote island,' I muttered casually. 'They should be sterilized to prevent them having any children.'

'Yoshioka-san, do you really mean that?' Mariko had been leaning back, but suddenly she sat upright and stared me straight in the eyes.

'Yes, I'm serious. There's nothing wrong with that, is there?'

'Yoshioka-san, you can be really heartless, can't you? Don't you feel sorry for those sick people at all?'

There was a tense silence between us for a while. But it did not last since, before long, we had reached the lights of Gotenba. For a start, what possible connection was there between us and the lepers? Their existence was totally divorced from our own. There was no point whatever in debating whether they required our sympathy or not.

However, by the time we reached Gotenba, Mariko had reverted to her previous good humour. I began joking with her and she covered her mouth with her hand as she laughed.

Back in Tokyo we all went our separate ways. The women all set off for home, but the group of single men were ready for more entertainment.

'I wouldn't mind a trip to the public baths.'

'Yes. Let's go to the Turkish baths.'

In response to this suggestion from someone in the group, we all decided to relieve our exhaustion in one of the Turkish baths that had just begun to appear in various parts of Tokyo at that time. Needless to say, this was combined with the dubious pleasure we could derive from having our backs massaged by those skimpily clad young ladies.

My diary (5)

The baths were located in Shinjuku, near the well-known Ka-buki-chō. It was easily recognizable from a distance because of the neon *Turkish Baths* sign that flickered on and off on the roof of the tiled building. At the top of the long deserted staircase leading up from the entrance that had been pointed out to us by a sandwich man, stood two men in bow-ties, their hands clasped in front of them.

'Welcome.'

We were all in lively good spirits, and when we hesitated at the entrance, the two men bowed to us in a manner reminiscent of hotel bell-boys. But there was an element of scorn in their attitude.

'Four for a bath, is it?' one of them asked. At this point he picked up the phone on his desk and came out with an order that, for some strange reason, was issued in English. 'Four baths, please.'

'Yes.' We could hear voices from within and a group of girls came out to meet us. They were dressed in dirty shorts and jackets. At first glance they could have been taken for pharmacists, but they were all short and plump. This, combined with their facial features, lent them the air of a group of crabs.

'The gentleman with glasses can take the bathroom to the right. The tall one in here. And you, sir, can have this room.' They had already decided on our nicknames and were assigning us to rooms located along both sides of the long, thin corridor.

'What's this? If you start giving us nicknames, it's just like the red-light district.'

In response, one of the girls said, 'Oh, sorry. It's not like that at all here. It's all perfectly healthy.' The girl laughed and pushed him by the shoulder.

But it was true. Because of their thick lipstick and their slovenly gait, one couldn't help being reminded of the women who worked in Kabuki-chō.

I was escorted by one of the girls into a room on the left at the end of the corridor. The room was divided into two sections. The first was the changing and massage areas and the other contained a small steam bath and a white-tiled, Western-style bath. The girl removed her jacket and hung it on the wall.

'Do you want to use the steam bath?'

Removing my tie, I stared at the girl in her bikini top and shorts.

'What are you staring at?' she asked. There was something over-deliberate about her question. But I had not been staring because I found her attractive. Her short, plump legs and her full waist were testimony to her rural upbringing. And there was a small red mark on one of her legs.

I had seen a body like that before. Not only had I seen it, I had embraced it with a mixture of disgust and passion. That was it! Mitsu! This girl was just like Mitsu. The two girls shared the same plump legs, thickset waist and, yes, that same ridiculously inane grin.

'Come on. What are you waiting for? Get in!' I was placed in the square, metal tub with only my neck protruding. I was to heat my entire body with the steam from the tub.

'I suppose you see all sorts of clients here, don't you?'

'Yes. There are the "salary men" like you. And then there are the old men.... But not so many young men. It's the forty- to fifty-year-olds we see most.'

My face was beginning to run with sweat from the steam and the girl set to work wiping my forehead and cheeks.

'I bet the forty-year-olds are a real pain, aren't they?' Turning my head from side to side, I suddenly came out with another question. 'Do they ever misbehave?'

The girl laughed out loud. It was the same inane guffaw that had been Mitsu's hallmark.

'Pass.'

'Come on. Tell us what they get up to.'

'I said, pass.' Her smile suggested she was used to the antics of middle-aged men and not in the least perturbed by them. I decided to try it on. But I was trapped in the steam bath and able to move my head only. I couldn't extract my hands or my feet. I felt just like a *daruma* doll, one of those squat, red Buddhist statues that the Japanese keep as good-luck symbols.

'"The sun sets over the mountains of Izu."' As she wiped my face with the towel the girl began to sing a popular song.

'Who sings that?'

'Oka Haruo.'

'Oh, that's right.'

It was then that I noticed the small chain she wore round her neck. There seemed to be something hanging from it, but it was hidden under her brassiere.

I crawled out of the steam bath and into the Western-style bath. After that, I returned to the changing-room and lay on my stomach to be massaged. The girl covered her hands with a white powder and massaged my neck, my shoulders and down my back.

'Come on, tell us!'

'Tell you what?'

'You know. What the middle-aged men get up to.' I stretched out my right hand and touched her shoulder. 'Is this it?'

'Stop it!'

'What's wrong.'

'I'll scream!'

The finger that touched her shoulder caught her chain and I caught sight of the greyish metal object that hung from it.

'What are you wearing? A locket with a photo of your lover?'

'No, it's not.'

I swallowed hard. The pendant was neither a locket nor a medal. It was a small, dirty crucifix. It was Mitsu's crucifix.

On the evening in Shibuya when I had been so angry, she

had followed me like a puppy. She had continually tried to humour me. But on seeing the old man standing there in the windswept station forecourt like a scarecrow, she had once more exposed that friendly streak of hers to the world. She had bought three cheap crucifixes and given one to me.

That evening crossed my mind like an ever-changing kaleidoscope. I was sure I had hurled that cross into the ditch that festered with discarded cigarette-ends and other scraps of rubbish. But that very same crucifix was now being worn by this girl at the Turkish baths.

'Hey, where did you buy this?'

'Wow, I'm scared. Why do you have to shout like that all of a sudden?'

'Where did you buy it?'

'I was given it.'

'By whom?'

'By a friend. A person who used to work here.' Her pronunciation of the word for 'person' marked her out as a Tokyoite.

'What was she called, this friend of yours?'

'Mitchan. Why do you ask? Do you know her?'

'Hey ... you don't mean, er ... Morita Mitsu, do you?'

'So you're Yoshioka-san, are you?' She stopped massaging and stared at me. Her expression had lost the familiarity, the wanton look it had evidenced until then, and for the first time she revealed the frightened look of a country girl. 'I see. So you're Yoshioka-san, are you? I see. Mitchan was always talking about you. Always. Always. ... '

The sound of a man and a woman laughing and of splashing water came wafting in from the next bathroom. They too were singing popular songs.

'Is she still here?'

'No, she left. She was here for half a year and then left. We used to work together.'

'Where is she now?'

'No idea. I did get a card from Kawasaki, but she didn't give any return address. She even mentioned you in that letter.'

'But there's nothing between us. Cut it out, will you? You're reading too much into things! It's nothing to do with me.'

'Really? I know it's none of my business, but Mitchan was really fond of you. And that never changed.'

'Well, that's up to her, isn't it?'

'But as I said . . . Mitsu left this job after getting caught up with some weird men. But even then, she insisted on giving me this just in case a man called Yoshioka-san showed up one day.' The girl was determined to make me understand Mitsu's feelings. But the more serious she became, the more obstinate I grew. My sense of self-respect was rocked by the realization that Mitsu had not forgotten me, but this was not sufficient to evoke in me feelings of sympathy for her. Rather, I felt as though weighed down by some troublesome burden. As I thought of Mitsu, I felt as if I were gazing through a veil of drizzle at a distant mountain range that is bathed in sunshine.

I stood up in silence and began to dress. The girl remained silent too. We could still hear the splashing and the sound of a man and a woman laughing in the next room.

'You're really cold, aren't you?'

Pushing open the door, I made to leave. At that moment, the girl muttered something. But it was hard to tell whether this was intended as a sigh or a deep breath.

'Poor . . . old . . . Mitchan.'

It was raining outside, a light drizzly rain.

I couldn't help feeling that Miura Mariko had come to feel something more than friendship for me. I had learnt from my experience with Mitsu how, when a woman begins to experience deeper feelings for a man, she becomes unbelievably devoted. The same applied to Mariko.

One day, on arrival at the office, I noticed that not only had the pencils and eraser on my desk been replaced, but the old abacus provided by the office had been changed into a new small one made of plain wood.

I wondered who had done that. But after I had looked around for a while, my gaze fell on Mariko who was sitting at the Japanese typewriter in the corner of the office. Of course she feigned ignorance. But even though her face may have given nothing away, there was something about the way she sat that betrayed her true feelings. 'How do you like your new abacus? Do you know who changed it for you?' The message was clear, even though she sat with her back to me. It was as though her back possessed its own powers of expression, its own mouth. She was wearing a cream-coloured dress.

'It was you, wasn't it?' I whispered to her as our paths crossed in the wash-room just before lunch.

'Umm . . . I wonder!' Mariko placed both hands on her head, laughed quietly and ran off.

But then equally suddenly, Mariko became incredibly distant. Looking all demure, she now refused to talk to me even when we did bump into each other. Remaining at her desk as though overwhelmed with work, she pointedly ignored me. And when work finished at five o'clock she would hurriedly place the cover on her typewriter and leave straight away. In retrospect, I can see that this change of attitude was simply a manifestation of the instinctive coquetry of young women; and yet, at the time, such behaviour induced in me not only a sense of jealousy but, equally, an unbearable fascination.

This one's quite different from Mitsu, I thought. In total contrast to Mitsu who, having fallen for me, ended up following me around like a lap-dog, Mariko's constantly evolving approach to life was refreshing and struck me as totally appropriate for a woman in contemporary society. In short, leaving aside my calculating approach towards a relative of the company chairman, I was infatuated.

One rainy evening I invited her to the movies after work. It was a British movie and so I knew that she would be interested. It was the story of an abortive love affair between a married woman and a doctor.

The cinema was crowded. There seemed no possibility of our securing seats, as even the area between the gallery and the exit was packed.

'This is hopeless,' she remarked.

'Shall we give it a miss? But what a waste of money! It's quite expensive, after all.'

'I was really looking forward to seeing the movie, too, you know,' Mariko muttered disconsolately.

Biting my nails, I suddenly came up with an idea. 'Right! I'll get you a seat within twenty minutes.'

'Don't be silly. That's impossible.'

'What will you do if I manage it?'

'Anything you say,' she replied with a smile.

Of course by 'anything' she meant treat me to a cup of tea or a cake after the movie – something ridiculous like that.

I dragged her to the entrance nearest to the screen. It was much less crowded here and I squeezed her between the people who were standing there.

'But I can't see,' she said.

'It's not the screen I'm worried about at the moment. I'm looking at the rows of seats. I'm going in there. When I raise my hand, you come over and join me.'

I eventually reached one of the rows of seats, but only after annoying those I had pushed against and treading on numerous feet. I knelt down in between the rows of seats and carefully observed the movements of those around me.

Fortunately for me, it was not ten minutes before one of the men in the row stood up. Securing the seat with the old newspaper I was carrying, I motioned to Mariko, who was looking over at me through the darkness.

'What cheek!' Someone was complaining behind me. But having secured the seat, it was ours to keep. Here too the 'winner takes all' approach, prominent throughout society, was in operation.

'How about it? I got you a seat.' I whispered to her as I sat her down.

'I'm amazed! You're so cheeky!'

'A promise is a promise. Don't forget!'

I was not in the least interested in the movie. What had the love affair of this married woman to do with me? For a start, I couldn't begin to comprehend why relationships between foreigners had to be so meticulously regulated. The man takes her to dinner. It was as though the only way the man could declare his love was to offer to light her cigarette and remove her coat in this reverential manner more reminiscent of a servant.

By comparison, the Japanese were far more impatient.

As we emerged into the night air at the end of the movie, I came straight to the point. 'Your seat was all thanks to my sweat and tears.'

'So what more do you want me to do to say thank you?'

'Well, you said that, if I found you a seat, you'd do anything.'

'Yes, that's right. A promise is a promise. What can I treat you to?'

'I don't want you to treat me to anything.' I spelt it out one word at a time. 'Let me kiss you.'

Mariko looked up at me in consternation. Then, averting her gaze, she continued. 'What beautiful shoes!'

She was looking at the shoes lined up in the shop window in front of us.

'How about it?'

But still there was no answer. I realized that, psychologically, it was far easier to tell someone you loved them than to demand something concrete like a kiss.

I escorted Mariko home to Ikebukuro on the national railway. In the train, I began whispering in her ear in keeping with the rhythm of the carriage. 'In the cinema, this shameless man . . .'

'What?'

' . . . fell in love with the girl he'd found a seat for. . . . He fell in love. Fell in love.'

The train rattled noisily along the line between Meguro and Shibuya. The rattling of the carriage and these expressions of love were in perfect synchrony.

'Well, did that girl . . . love him? Did she?' I gently poked Mariko in the ribs as I spoke.

Some of the passengers, exhausted from a hard day's work, had shut their eyes, some were reading the sports paper. They remained totally oblivious of the love charade that was secretly taking place between Mariko and myself. Outside, we could see the rows of small, dirty houses, dimly lit windows and the silhouettes of families gathered around the table for their meagre evening meal. But, equally suddenly, they disappeared from view.

'Did she love him? Did she?'

Mariko placed her finger on the steamed-up window. 'Yes.' Like an aeroplane creating a vapour trail, she wrote the three letters of the English affirmative. At the same time, a wonderful feeling of self-esteem welled up slowly from the depths of my being.

'And in the end, she too....'

I savoured the sensation as one relishes to the full that last morsel which one has kept back till the end.

It was just at that moment. The train had just entered the outskirts of Shibuya and, in my exultation, my eye was drawn to the night lights of Dōgenzaka and the red and blue neon signs of the cinemas. Directly behind these lay that place – of course, it was enveloped in darkness – but that unforgettable place where I had first held Mitsu, the inn, the hill, the railway siding... all these now bore down on my senses.

Suddenly, the image of Mitsu pierced my heart like a nail. I could not explain it. Was it because, in comparison with the bright lights of the main street of Shibuya, this one area struck me at the time as dark, forlorn and depressing? I could not explain it. Was it because I had superimposed this dark, forlorn and depressing area on to the image of Morita Mitsu? I could not explain it. Was it because, whilst I had come to find happiness in my work and with Mariko, that girl had disappeared without a trace, leaving only that cross in the Turkish bath?

The train entered Shibuya Station. A crowd of people surged on to the platform, to be replaced on the train by another crowd of people, their faces betraying a deep-rooted weariness. As the doors closed with a squeak, I found myself recalling the look on Mitsu's face that day on this same platform as she chased after the train, as though trying to cling to it.

'Are you tired?' Mariko leant against me and whispered in my ear. 'You're really strange, suddenly going all quiet like this.'

'What? No, I'm not tired.'

'You sometimes look really sad, you know.'

'You must be joking. I'm not all sentimental like that. I hate sentimental people!'

We tried to keep it secret. But our fellow-workers – especially those hypersensitive young women – were vaguely aware of the relationship between Mariko and myself. It was probably only the chairman and the two executive directors who remained unaware.

At first, it was greeted with comments from my male colleagues that betrayed a tinge of jealousy and a somewhat spiteful cynicism. There were times during coffee-breaks when a group of them would be gathered around someone's desk deep in conversation, only to cease abruptly when I approached. They must have been talking about us. Sometimes – of course, this was only when Mariko was out of the office – they would make deliberately audible comments such as, 'I wonder if they've kissed?'

'Of course they have. After all. . . . '

This would be followed by stifled laughter.

Right, if that's the way they want it, I thought to myself, I'll show them! Both at work and outside, I began to act in a way designed to acknowledge Mariko as my girl-friend. At first our colleagues were taken aback, but before long they came to accept it. They were probably aware that, since Mariko was the chairman's relative, it was in their better interests to stay on good terms with me. Eventually the caustic remarks and snide comments stopped. But still they continued to stare at us out of curiosity.

'I wonder if they've kissed?'

But the fact of the matter was that Mariko and I had yet to exchange our first kiss.

I suppose I respected Mariko. I was the kind of man who had felt no compunction in taking advantage of someone like Mitsu. So why was I so considerate of Mariko's lips and her purity?

I have to admit, this was partly due to the fact that I was reluctant to lose her trust. If I were to lose her trust and our love were destroyed, I would become a laughing-stock amongst my colleagues and would end up being treated with disdain, even by the company executives.

But for all that I was a young man. As we walked together, I would be overcome with a desire to touch her, to hold her close to me. When our knees happened to collide as we sat in the coffee shop, I was acutely aware of the soft warmth of her body transmitted from her knee to mine. And there were those times as she suddenly leant against me on the train when I would be conscious of the smell of her hair or sense her breasts brushing against my hands.

All this I endured. And, in retrospect, I feel I did well to resist.

'Yoshioka-san, you are forever making crude remarks, but deep down you're innocent, aren't you?' There was deep feeling in Mariko's voice as she made this comment one rainy day in the coffee shop.

'Hmm. I wonder?'

'I like people like that. That's why I feel safe with you, even late at night.'

'Don't forget I'm a man. But as Marx said, when in love, one shouldn't breach the line designed not to be breached. I'm in full agreement with Marx on that one.'

'I'm impressed. You're always quoting the positive side of Marxist ideology.'

'Hmm, you think so? I'm not so sure. But I have read a lot of Marx.'

However, there was one secret I kept from Mariko. There were two or three occasions when, after leaving her following a date, I ended up in the red-light district. I needed some way of relieving the feelings that Mariko aroused in me and I decided to turn to the 'women of the night' for this purpose.

I felt no inherent contradiction in turning to such women for the relief of my feelings of passion, leaving my own girlfriend untouched. I certainly did not look on my actions as in any way deceiving Mariko. Of course I told Mariko nothing of these excursions, but this was because I feared that a young girl like her would not understand the physiological needs of a young man and would simply dismiss them as 'dirty'. To be perfectly honest, I had come to divide women into two categories, and what was not permissible with women from category A, was perfectly acceptable with women from category B. Mariko belonged to category A. The women of the red-light district and Morita Mitsu I assigned to category B.

One rainy day, after escorting Mariko as far as Ikebukuro, I was overcome by an insatiable urge. As we walked the streets that evening, my feelings of excitement were aroused by the thin, cream-coloured nylon blouse Mariko was wearing. Massaging her shoulder as we sat in the coffee shop, she had remarked, 'I'm tired. I've been typing all day.' Then, fixing me with a teasing look, she had continued, 'When you're married, will you massage your wife's shoulders?'

'Yes, of course. But I wonder who that might be!' I replied.

'I don't know. I wonder!' There was a distinctly coquettish note to her voice and a twinkle in her eye as she spoke. I was overwhelmed by a surge of emotion and stared at the floor. A fine drizzle was falling outside and the coffee shop was saturated with a muggy heat. The unusually sticky atmosphere may have had something to do with my excitement. I found myself looking at her legs and, before I knew what was happening, I was picturing first the calves and knees that were concealed by her stockings and then her thighs.

Such thoughts remained imprinted on my mind even after I boarded the train and I was soon cursing Marx for having devised a set of values that was so difficult to live up to.

I left the train at Shinjuku, planning to dismiss such ideas from my head with a glass of *shōchū* at one of the open-air stalls.

I downed a glass of a cheap, pink-coloured drink made from grapes at a roadside stall outside the west exit of the station. But the oppressive atmosphere and the warming effect of the drink served only to enhance my emotions. I realized that this oppressive mugginess was the most effective stimulant of the male physiology.

I walked towards the Turkish baths I had visited the other day with my colleagues. As I passed in front of the baths, I was fortunately too relaxed from the drink to start troubling myself with thoughts of Morita Mitsu again.

I crossed the main road and entered the red-light district. The road would have made a perfect film location as it stretched out in the drizzle as far as the eye could see. It was lined on both sides with houses that resembled tiny cake-boxes and in front of each door stood a couple of girls soliciting custom. Their cheeks wet from the rain, they invited me inside.

'Wow. You look just like Sata Keiji!' One of the women who looked particularly gaunt ran out into the rain and leant on my arm in an attempt to pull me inside.

'Hey! Stop messing me about!' I shouted.

'What do you mean? I'll rip your clothes if you try and run off!'

Relieved of my shoes and pushed from behind, I eventually followed her up the stairs into a small room. It was a six-mat room furnished with only a dresser and a tea cupboard. Through the window I could see the pale-red glow of the neon sign opposite. That was the Turkish baths. The Turkish baths where Mitsu used to work. She too must have looked at the neon glow in the night sky on evenings like this.

As I lay with the girl, my thoughts did not turn to Mariko. That is part of the male psychology. It is easy for young men to divorce physiology from psychology in a way that is not so easy for girls. Woman are attracted only to those whom they love. But men are able to differentiate between an object of love and an object of passion. Mariko was Mariko. This girl was this girl.

As the evening developed, we heard the sound of the street

vendor's flute and of drunks singing as they passed under our window. Eventually, all was quiet. Having succumbed to my caresses, the girl fell asleep with her mouth agape. Her breath was stale and she looked generally exhausted.

A new day dawned. The sun filtered through the tiny cracks between the shutters. The girl was still asleep and so I lit a cigarette and opened the window. I could see another 'woman of the night' hanging a *futon* up to dry at the window opposite. Her client must have left already. Her hair was done up with a series of pins and she smiled at me as our eyes met. As she did so, her golden fillings sparkled in the sunlight.

'I'm going. Hey, wake up!'

'What? You're going already? You're early.' She scratched her slender arms as she followed me down the staircase. She had lost one of her slippers and dragged the other along the floor in a most slovenly fashion.

Somehow everything struck me as dirty. The women, this house, the street . . . they all appeared sullied. I was eager to leave the scene and make for the main road as quickly as possible. I was still in time for work.

'Hey!' There was no denying the voice behind me. Turning round, I recognized Ono, one of my colleagues from work.

'Hey, Yoshioka-san. What are you doing in a place like this?' A sarcastic grin played across Ono's lips. 'Are you sure it's OK? Are you sure it's OK if Mariko finds out?'

I remained silent. I was overcome by the realization that I had landed myself in a most unfortunate predicament.

My diary (6)

Throughout that day as I sat at my desk I felt as though my whole body were pierced with nails. The entire office was aware of the relationship between Mariko and me and it was an open secret that, sooner or later, we would marry. Since Mariko was the chairman's niece, the probability that I would eventually join the executive board of the company was the source of considerable resentment and jealousy amongst my colleagues.

So what would happen if news of my exploits in the red-light district of Shinjuku the previous evening were to be spread by Ono? The female employees would no doubt look on me as a feckless man who had betrayed his girl-friend by taking another woman. And they would not stop at me. They would probably stare at Mariko with that look of scorn that is reserved for members of the same sex.

'Hey, Mari-chan hasn't noticed anything! She's too full of herself!' I felt as though I could hear such comments being made in whispered tones during the lunch-break in the wash-room and corridors.

And my male colleagues would presumably start making comments such as, 'You see! She still won't give herself to him!'

'That's right. That's why. . . .'

Looking up from my desk, I looked over at Mariko. I was sure she had not yet heard anything from Ono. As usual, she was gazing down at her keyboard, typing away in that earnest manner of hers. It was early summer and already there were traces of sweat on her cheeks.

With a pencil in his mouth, Ono was fingering his abacus.

On finishing his calculation, he recorded something on his notepad and suddenly removed a matchbox from his pocket. He started removing wax from his ear with a match and assiduously placing it on his notepad.

How filthy, I thought. That's disgusting.

It was not that he heard my tongue clicking in disapproval, but at that moment Ono suddenly looked up. Then, as our eyes met, a smile suddenly drifted across that pale face with the shifty eyes. Then, still smiling, he looked over at Mariko in a very deliberate manner.

It was perfectly clear what was implied by that gesture. It was obviously designed to remind me of the incident that morning and to inform me that it was entirely up to me whether or not Mariko be appraised of the truth.

And that was not the end of the matter. That day during the lunch-break I was troubled by a further development.

'Hey, Yoshioka-san.' I had just emerged from the wash-room when Ono came up to me with his customary smile and said, 'I have a small request.'

'Well, what is it, then?' I braced myself, like a boxer awaiting the bell.

'I've lost a lot of money at mah-jong. Can you lend me a bit?'

'Money?' But I'm broke myself! And it's not pay-day yet.'

'That's odd! You had enough to go off to the red-light district.' Ono stared at me as he spoke in measured tones. 'Or did you perhaps borrow that money from your lover? In which case, it won't matter if I talk to Miura-san about it, will it?'

'How much do you want?' My voice quavered, betraying a mixture of anger and contempt.

'Three thousand yen... no, two thousand will do.'

'All right. I'll bring it tomorrow.'

'Tomorrow? You mean, you haven't got it on you? Can't be helped, I suppose. OK. Don't forget, though!' As he disappeared down the corridor humming a popular tune, Ono wore an expression that suggested he was quite justified in extorting money from me.

As it happens, since it was right before pay-day, I had less than a thousand yen in my pocket. I could probably raise the money somehow, but my self-esteem would never allow me to borrow it from Mariko as Ono had suggested. I was still loath to expose the more unseemly aspects of my nature to Mariko.

That afternoon I stayed in the office, but there was no alleviating my feelings of melancholy. Returning home, I sat down by the window and stared absently at the pinkish clouds over the sheet-iron roof as I strove desperately to come up with a suitable plan of action.

I resolved never to visit the red-light district again. I was to blame for dropping my guard. And I wouldn't let Ono get any further with his attempts to take advantage of human frailty. I would lend him two thousand yen this time, but if ever he tried to make light of me again, I would not take it lying down. Who did he take this Yoshioka Tsutomu for? The very thought of Ono made my blood boil as though my entire being were given over to alcohol.

But if I were to renounce the red-light district, how was I to satisfy my youthful urges? Should I take my courage in both hands and tell Mariko? No, no! What if this happened to incite in her feelings of contempt? It was all too clear how the chairman and the directors, Yoshimura-san and Kataoka-san, would look on me in such circumstances. In which case, what was I to do?

It was at this moment that I recalled Mitsu with her ridiculous, good-natured smile. Maybe she still loved me. In which case I could turn to her instead of heading off to the red-light district. She may have been short and fat. But were the girls in the red-light district so very different?

With that thought, I sensed a gradual dissipation of the melancholy mood that had overwhelmed me throughout the day. I changed, left my apartment and took the Metropolitan line. It was some time since I had last visited Kim-san's office in Jinbōchō but, just as I had always turned to him when in need of cash as a student, so now I was looking to him to help me out with the two thousand yen I needed by the following day.

I could still recall that autumn evening two years ago when I first visited Swan Industrial. The one small block that had been spared the ravages of war enveloped in mist and the children playing catch in the alley. The house with the charcoal brazier giving off a thin cloud of smoke. And hadn't there been an old man who rode by on his squeaky old bicycle who went round performing impromptu shows using picture stories? There was no doubt about it... I had been much poorer and hungrier in those days.

I could see Kim-san moving about behind the glass door. Still dressed like an actor in a second-rate movie, he was talking to a man in a livery coat whom I took for an employee.

I greeted Kim-san as I opened the door and, as I did so, Kim-san turned round and broke into a broad smile.

'Hey, it's you!'

'Long time, no see.'

'Yes.... You look well. And there's colour in your cheeks. You must be earning well and eating well! I can tell just by looking at your clothes.'

'No.' I gently shook my head. 'That's not altogether true. Actually, I've come about money again.'

'You're *stupit*! Real *stupit*! What do you use it on? Ah-ha! I bet I can guess!'

'No, it's not that. I just want to borrow two thousand yen if possible.'

Regardless of his attitude towards others, Kim-san was always cordial with me. He must have had an innate sense that I was a young Japanese man whom he had taken under his wing. He had this tendency always to lecture me in his broken Japanese, but I was strangely attracted to him.

In return for my promise to repay the two thousand yen on pay-day the following month, Kim-san promptly drew the money from his trouser pocket and handed it over to me, saying, 'I've set up a large office in Kawasaki. I've sold this place and will be moving soon.' With great relish, he explained how his operations had expanded, that he had acquired a pachinko parlour in Kawasaki and planned to turn the second floor of that building into the office for Swan Industrial.

'In Kawasaki?'

'Yes, that's right. There are thousands of Koreans working in Kawasaki. Some have opened *pars*. Others are running Turkish *paths*. And they're all doing well. The *Chapanese* are hopeless! Too cowardly!'

Mention of the words 'Turkish baths' and of Kawasaki served to jog something in my memory. As I stood there smoking one of Kim-san's cigarettes, I thought of Mitsu. Yes ... if there were any truth in what the girl at the Turkish baths in Shinjuku had told me, then Mitsu had gone off to Kawasaki.

'By the way, Kim-san, I've got one more favour to ask.'

'What is it? More money?'

'No. I want you to help me find someone. A girl called Morita Mitsu.'

I could see the knowing sparkle in Kim-san's eyes through his glasses.

'Oh, I see.' Raising one finger, he continued. 'I see. A girlfriend, is it?'

I was on the verge of denying it, but ended up just smiling. That seemed a better way of handling the situation.

'Where's she living, this *cirl* of yours?'

'I don't know. But I think she's working in either a Turkish baths or a pachinko parlour, like those run by your friends. I know it's like looking for a needle in a haystack, but ...'

'I see.' This time, Kim-san stared at my wrist without any show of emotion. 'This could be quite *tifficult*.'

Just as I was leaving, Kim-san suddenly called me back, stretched out his hand and asked for something by way of collateral.

'Collateral?'

'Yes. You've borrowed two thousand yen, so I need some *carantee*. I'll *cive* it back when you pay me back.'

'Oh, come on, Kim-san. Don't you trust me?'

'You *Chapanese* are all the same. A contract is a contract. I trust money more than people.'

Kim-san was clearly in no mood to concede and he ended up relieving me of my cheap Japanese watch by way of security.

Glancing around him, Ono quickly pocketed the two thousand yen with a nervous smile.

'Sorry about this.'

'That's your lot. No more!'

'Yes, I know. You don't need to tell me that.'

'Well, sorry to labour the point, but it's only this once. I hate borrowing, but I also hate lending money.'

'OK. There's no need to be so cold about it.' Bathed in the sunshine that was streaming through the window, Ono's face wore an expression of cowardly smugness. On the one hand, I felt a sense of relief that I had finally extricated myself from a difficult situation, but I was still slightly concerned about what he might try next.

When I returned to the office, Mariko stopped typing and smiled. My other colleagues, too, were all acting perfectly normally. I inferred from this that Ono had yet to divulge our secret.

But that was all because of the two thousand yen. I determined not to push him to return the money. It was better to leave him in my debt. That was the best way to keep him quiet. It would hurt to have to hand over part of my monthly salary to Kim-san in return for my watch. But I had to convince myself that that was the price I had to pay to secure Ono's silence.

Kim-san was a great believer in contracts, and it therefore came as no surprise that he kept his side of the bargain. He had not seemed particularly taken by my request at the time, but some two weeks later he telephoned me to report on Mitsu.

'It was really *tifficult* to find out anything about it, but I managed.'

'About what?'

'Oh, you're *stupit*! About the woman. Your lady-friend!'

'Oh, I see! ... My lady-friend!' Glancing cautiously at Mariko and my other colleagues, I hurriedly lowered my voice. According to Kim-san, one of his fellow-Koreans who was running a pachinko parlour had employed Mitsu. But she was no longer there. She had been fired.

'Why was she fired?'

'She was taking money from the till. Helped herself, then *tisappeared*.'

'Who? Mitsu?!' I was taken aback. That pathetic little girl had been stealing? She always looked so kind-hearted and I tried to imagine how she could have sunk to stealing.

That was the extent of Kim-san's knowledge of the matter, but he agreed to introduce me to his friend if I were willing to accompany him to Kawasaki.

'Are you coming?'

'All right. I'll go with you tonight.' I replaced the receiver and wiped the sweat from my brow. Nobody suspected anything. Mariko was looking down at her desk and Ono was studying some documents, extracting wax from his ears with a match as he did so. I was interested – perhaps curious is not too strong a word – to learn how Mitsu had stolen the money. I felt as though I could almost picture her tentatively stretching out a hand to the till.

'What a fool!' I muttered to myself. 'What a fool!'

There are people in this world who, though basically well meaning, deliberately place themselves on the slippery slope. These are the people who, through their own ineptitude and lack of tact, are unable to distinguish between acceptable and unacceptable behaviour. Mitsu must have belonged to that category of person.

After work, Mariko placed the cover on her typewriter, put her fingers in her hair and smiled at me. This was the code that the two of us had developed, designed to suggest that we go out together that evening.

In retrospect, it was a great mistake to reject this suggestion. But maybe things would have turned out as they did sooner or later, even if we had gone out together that evening.

The station square in Kawasaki was enveloped in the evening mist and I was constantly jostled by the hordes of people emerging from the ticket-barrier. I couldn't help wondering if Mitsu was caught up in this crowd. It had been a lovely clear day, but there was just a hint of rain in the sky now.

I spotted the new Swan Industrial building almost immediately. A whole series of wreaths to celebrate the opening of business had been set up in front of the pachinko parlour and people must have been attracted by the new design of machine that allowed for continuous play because, beneath the strong fluorescent lights, there was a crowd of men and women riveted to the tiny balls inside the machines. The interior of the parlour reverberated to the strains of a popular song. I had heard that song somewhere before.

'I wonder where she's living now
That girl I left behind that day.
I wonder what she's doing now.'

Kim-san was slowly walking around amongst the customers listening to the music and giving advice to the girls who were handing out the prizes. There was a look of evident satisfaction in his eyes as he greeted me with a smile.

'I wonder where she's living now
That girl I left behind that day.
I wonder what she's doing now.'

'You're really taken by that *cirl*, aren't you?'
'Don't be stupid!'
'That's why you came round here so quickly, isn't it? Look, you've *con* all red. You're so naïve, aren't you!'
'Give us a break! Anyway, where's this friend of yours?'
'His shop's really close. Do you want to go and see? I've told him to expect us, so let's go.'

This latest pachinko parlour was very similar to the one run by Kim-san, but it was poorly lit, the machines were old and there was only a handful of customers.

I bought twenty yen's worth of balls, stood in front of one of the machines whose spring had long since ceased to function smoothly and operated the starting button in a perfunctory manner. The balls themselves seemed disinterested as they struck the bent nails, rebounded and then disappeared into the receptacle at the bottom like those who have drifted from the mainstream of life. Watching the pathetic balls one by one, I couldn't help viewing this as a reflection of life.

'Hey, that machine....' Sucking a cherry, a girl in glasses whispered to me from behind. 'If you use that one, you're bound to lose. That one over there's much better.'

'Thank you. But if you tell all your customers that, you're the ones who'll lose out.'

'So what? What does it matter to me if the parlour loses out?'

'Hey, there was a girl called Morita who used to work here, wasn't there?' I gave the name slowly as though reciting it from memory and immediately the girl stared at me with a start. It reminded me of the girl in the Turkish baths two months earlier.

'Do you know... Mitchan?'

'Yes. I used to. I hear she left. Pilfering money from the till, wasn't she?'

'She didn't take anything.' The way in which she drew up her shoulders suggested she was angry. 'She was just trying to help... Baba-san.'

'Eh? What do you mean? This is getting complicated.'

The girl emerged from between two pachinko machines. She was wearing geta.[1] Still noisily sucking on the cherry, she gazed all around and continued, 'I mean... the owner of this place is really stingy. Baba-san is living all alone with her brother who has spinal caries. She has to pay for everything – his medicines, his doctor's bills. They're all costly. But because

1. Japanese-style clogs

she'd already had several loans, she couldn't borrow any more from the owner. And so she ended up taking some from the till.'

'And she was caught?'

'Yes. But because Mitchan was living alone at the time, she decided to take responsibility for it ... and told the owner *she'd* done it.'

'I suppose she was taken to the police, was she?'

'No. The owner's been involved in all sorts of incidents in the past, so I suppose he didn't want the publicity.'

'Was the money returned?'

'Yes. The owner made her work in a bar until she had paid back the lot.'

'Does she sometimes come back here?'

'Only once. I want to see her ... but it's the sort of seedy bar where girls can't go.'

Outside, a light drizzle was falling. A young man was hurriedly moving a bicycle that had been parked in the road to a more sheltered spot. He then started to whistle.

Having ascertained the name and location of the bar, I left the parlour. The rain pricked the nape of my neck and my face. I wanted to say goodbye to Kim-san, but he was nowhere to be seen in the shop. All that could be heard was the continued clatter of pachinko balls and the same song emerging from the loudspeakers.

So, she had moved from a pharmaceutical company to Turkish baths, then on to a pachinko parlour, and now finally to a 'seedy bar', had she?

> 'I wonder what she's doing now.
> There's no way of knowing.'

The lyrics of that song appeared to be hounding me. It really was nothing to do with me what she was doing with her life, but I was coming to realize that men are liable to experience a wave of sentimentality on learning that a woman from their past is struggling to find her feet in life.

That was it. At that moment, I betrayed a sentimentality that was totally out of character. My cheeks and face were damp from the drizzle and I was biting my fingers as I walked, but I couldn't help thinking about the life of that girl who, until that moment, had rarely entered my thoughts. Just like those pachinko balls striking those nails, rebounding and then falling, so too Mitsu had fallen. I wondered why she had not been more successful in negotiating a steady path through life as I had. She had taken the sins of others upon herself and deliberately wreaked havoc on her own destiny. That ridiculous manner of speaking of hers! The way in which her sympathy had prompted her to devote herself to me wholeheartedly on learning about my childhood polio. There was no hope for someone like that!

The narrow, rain-drenched street was lined on both sides with bars where only the façade had been finished with concrete and paint. The bars bore names such as Julie and Lily of the Valley and other commonplace flowers, and the fact that these were written up using *katakana* characters[2] lent them a vaguely foreign air. There was not a single customer in the street and on hearing my footsteps a young girl opened the door and looked out. 'Won't you come in?' she inquired.

It was just like the red-light district of Shinjuku. Maybe these bars were engaged in the same line of business?

'Come on, it's cheap.'

I could hear hoarse male voices coming from inside.

'What are you talking about... with a face like that! And I bet the service you offer is pathetic!'

I stopped in front of the 'Saffron' where Mitsu worked and again I was greeted from out of the darkness by a woman.

'How about a beer?'

'Only if Mitchan's there.'

'Mitchan?'

'Yes, that's right.'

2. One of the two Japanese syllabaries, usually used to transcribe imported words

114

'There's no one of that name here. But I'll look after you instead. Come in.'

'I'm talking about Morita Mitsu.'

'Oh, I see. You mean Sakiko.' Apparently Mitsu worked under the name Sakiko in this bar. 'She's off today.'

'Off work? Is she sick?'

'She's gone to hospital.'

'What's wrong with her?'

'I'm not sure. She's probably gone to have treatment for that spot of hers.... Come on. What's it matter if Sakichan's not here? Come on in!'

'My name's Yoshioka.' I handed her a piece of paper with my name and address. 'Please tell her I dropped in.'

Realizing that I was not about to enter, the girl launched into a tirade of insults.

'So she's sick, is she?' I was overcome by a wave of fatigue. For some reason, I felt exhausted, not just physically, but right to the depths of my being. A solitary dog staggered across the road through the rain.

At that moment I felt as though someone were whispering in my ear. I am still unable to explain why I should have heard that voice at that instant.

'If you hadn't met her that day,' the voice muttered, 'she might have led a very different life – a much happier, more uneventful life.'

'It's not my fault.' I shook my head. 'If we spent all our time thinking like that, we'd end up meeting nobody. We wouldn't be able to get on with our daily lives, would we?'

'That's true. That's part of the complexity of life. But never forget! It's not possible for someone to interact with a fellow human being without leaving some traces.'

I shook my head and continued to walk through the rain. Just as I had that evening in Shibuya when I had walked off towards the station without a thought for Mitsu who was following me like a puppy.

But the following day the rain had cleared up, the sun was

shining and I had quite forgotten both Mitsu and the uncharacteristic wave of sentimentality that had been elicited by thoughts of her.

Right! Back to work! You have absolutely no connection with girls like that whose lives are plummeting like falling pebbles. Or so the brilliant sky and dazzling sunshine of early summer seemed to be telling me.

I applied myself to my work with unprecedented enthusiasm. I greeted everyone – yes, even Ono – with a friendly disposition, worked diligently and kept asking Yoshimura-san to sign more documents.

'Where did you go last night?' Mariko asked me during the lunch-break as we walked together along the sunny street. The leaves of the ginkgo trees at the side of the road had been well nourished by the June rains and were a deep green colour. 'I was really bored.'

'I'm sorry.' I was always gentle with Mariko. 'I had something I just had to do. I just couldn't get out of it.'

'I ended up going to the place where I used to work, because there was nothing else to do.'

'Where was that?'

'Didn't I tell you? Before coming to my uncle's company, I worked for a while at a pharmaceutical firm in Kyōdō. I thought that was a good way to see the real world. But it was small and dingy, so I soon left.'

'Really?' I tried to sound unconcerned, but my voice was quivering. 'That must have been fun.'

'There weren't many people I knew there. There were two other girls there with me, but they have both left.' She was rambling on about her past. It was as though revealing her past in this way was proof of her trust and affection for me. But I found it too painful.

'Shall we go and listen to some jazz at Roxy's?' I hurriedly changed the subject. But Mariko was oblivious to this.

'Is someone singing?'

'Oh no, I can't. I haven't got any money left.'

'How could you? You went off drinking without telling me

last night, didn't you? You can't do that when we're married. OK, I'll treat you to a cup of tea.'

We ended up listening to some light music in a shop called Silver Paris on the Ginza. That was a good place to enjoy a cup of tea and hear a few young singers.

Two days passed. Three days. Ono showed no signs of threatening me again.

I felt as though I had resolved everything smoothly when, on returning home from work about a week later, I noticed a postcard that had been thrown on to the letter-rack by the front door. I recognized those clumsy characters as Mitsu's. They reminded me of a child's handwriting: 'How are you doing? I was very surprised to hear that you had come to our place. Please don't be angry. But I don't want you to come again. It can't be helped. I've had this problem quite some time now and. . . .'

As always, her writing was full of mistaken characters and others that had been completely omitted. But the letter evidenced a new sense of loneliness and despair.

The following evening I phoned from Kawasaki Station and asked for Mitsu. I was not without some sympathy and curiosity at the prospect of meeting Mitsu after all this time. That was a genuine feeling, but so too was my intention of using her as a substitute for the girls in Shinjuku.

I can still vividly recall the scene. Once again, a light drizzle was falling.

I smoked a cigarette as I waited for her in Rocky, a coffee shop near the station. I had just received my pay-packet and so my wallet was full.

And it was not just my wallet that was full. I was feeling incredibly magnanimous. Depending on her condition, I was even contemplating giving her some pocket-money and something warm to eat. I suppose I was seeking to assuage the guilty conscience I nourished towards her in this way.

I waited twenty minutes. But Mitsu failed to turn up. On the phone she had sounded very sad and I had struggled to persuade her to meet me. Ever since that evening in Shibuya,

I had known how to convince her to do something. She was inherently incapable of turning her back on the pain and misery of another. And yet, even after thirty minutes, there was still no sign of her.

I suppose she's finally come to hate me after all. Even a worm has its pride! I decided to give her forty minutes and then leave.

Just at that moment, a small shadow appeared at the door. Her face and hair were drenched from the rain and she stood there staring vacantly through the window holding a battered umbrella. She reminded me of an abandoned cat. She had no raincoat and was wearing *geta*. As always her hair was done up in three plaits.

Mitsu stared straight at me. I had seen those eyes before. It was the same as the look I had seen that time on the platform at Shibuya Station as, having watched the doors close, she had run after the train straining desperately to catch sight of me.

'How are you? I came looking for you the other day.'

The waitress came over to take our orders and stared at Mitsu. Even after the coffee had arrived, Mitsu just gazed at the table and made no attempt to drink.

'What's the matter? I came round because I was missing you. Don't you want to come out with me this evening? Eh? Come on. Let's do something together, just like the good old days! That evening in Shibuya was fun, wasn't it? Do you still remember that bar with all the singing? And that old palmist who came up to you?... What's up? Do you want to be left alone? You've come to hate me, haven't you?'

At that moment, Mitsu finally raised her head and looked at me.

'You have, haven't you?'

'No, it's not that. It's not that.' Her face was rather contorted and she was on the verge of tears as she sobbed. 'I like you.'

'If you like me, why won't you come out with me?'

'Because I . . .'

'Are you going to tell me you can't because you work in

the bar? What's it matter? That makes it easier for me, too.'

'I'm ... sick.'

It was only now that I noticed that she was incredibly pale. 'Sick? What's wrong? It's not TB, is it?'

'No, it's not. I had the doctor look at the spot on my arm. . . .'

'And?'

'He said I need a full examination. So I'm going to Gotenba the day after tomorrow.'

'Gotenba?'

'Yes.' Mitsu broke off for a second. 'There's a special hospital there.'

I suddenly recalled the bus journey back from Lake Yamanaka that evening with Mariko and the rest of the company and the hospital we had seen in the distance. A lonely hospital, miles from anywhere, in the middle of a wood. If my memory served me correctly, it was a leprosarium.

'What?! You're joking.'

I tried vaguely to reassure her, but then Mitsu held her hands to her head ... and cried.

The spot on the wrist (2)

Four days before her meeting with Yoshioka-san, Mitsu had gone to the university hospital. It had been another drizzly day, just like the day they had met.

During the course of the past month or so she had been aware of a slight swelling around the dark spot on her wrist. It was only about the size of a ten-yen coin, and didn't hurt even if someone pushed or bumped against it. And yet the swelling appeared to be growing steadily in size.

'What's this? It looks horrible.' It was a casual remark made one evening by a middle-aged man who had noticed the spot while toying with Mitsu's arm during a drinking session. 'Is it a growth?' The man ran a shoe shop in Kawasaki. He was rather too susceptible to his drink, and the other girls all disapproved of him, but for some reason he was always considerate to Mitsu. 'You'd better get this seen to, or your customers won't like it. It's OK this time because it's me, but next time...'

'I've been putting ointment on it , but it's not getting any better.'

'Medicine over the counter is useless. Quite useless.' The man held Mitsu's hand up to the light and squinted as he looked at it as though staring at some distant object. 'If there's one thing you have to get properly treated in a hospital, it's skin disease.'

Under the reddish light in the bar, the spot on her wrist appeared darker than usual and the surrounding skin glistened like the trail left by a snail.

After the middle-aged client had left, another man named Tada-san arrived to take his place. He had been deserted by his wife some two months previously and when he came to the bar he did nothing but air his complaints. The other girls tended to make fun of this wan, thin company man and Mitsu was the only one willing to entertain him. He constantly regaled her with tales of his unfortunate plight, but Mitsu couldn't help but feel sorry for him as he spoke.

This man, too, noticed the dark spot. He twisted away from her as though he had just set eyes on something terrifying or dirty.

'Is it one of those?'

'What do you mean, "one of those"?' In her naïvety, Mitsu could only question him with a look of blank amazement. She resembled a tiny bird that had been struck by a peanut.

'You know. The disease we Japanese call "plum poisoning".'

The girls at the counter burst out laughing, but still Mitsu failed to comprehend.

'Mitchan, you really must go to the doctor's. The man who runs the shoe shop said the same thing, didn't he?' The remark was made by one of the other girls, Yoshie, who was cleaning her teeth with a toothpick.

'But it doesn't hurt and doesn't itch.'

'That may be OK with you. But what if we catch it?'

Mitsu blushed and looked down. She began to rub the floor with her feet.

The next day she went to the local clinic run by Dr Shirai. It was a small, grubby clinic next to the pawnbroker's. In addition to general medicine it also specialized in paediatrics, venereology and dermatology. It was a hot, muggy day and the doctor who was plump and bald wore a dirty physician's coat over a track suit. The waiting-room was a small four and a half mat affair by the entrance with yellowing magazines and children's picture-books scattered about. While awaiting her turn, Mitsu looked after the child of the woman who had arrived before her. The woman coughed drily as she spoke. 'I'm sorry, Will you keep an eye on him for a while?' So saying, she entered the consulting-room.

The boy was about five years old and he stared intently at

Mitsu, his face smeared from his runny nose.

'What's your name?'

'Tsutomu.'

Mitsu immediately recalled that this was Yoshioka's name. She wondered whether Yoshioka knew of her move to Kawasaki. She wanted to meet him. She desperately wanted to meet him, if only once more.

'Let's just wait here quietly. Nice and quietly. Your mother will soon be finished.' She was trying to keep him happy with words that took her back to her own childhood. Just wait quietly. Nice and quietly. That summed up her attitude towards Yoshioka. Not just towards Yoshioka: it summed up her attitude towards all her acquaintances.

'Where's Mum?'

'She'll soon be finished.'

The mother was escorted to the door of the consulting-room by the doctor. She was still coughing drily.

'We'll have to take an X-ray. I can definitely hear a murmur. Otherwise I'll contact the health centre.... Next please.'

There was an all-pervading smell of body odour and disinfectant in the dark consulting-room as the doctor examined the dark spot on Mitsu's wrist. Mitsu could see some sunflowers outside the window and she could hear the little boy crying.

'How long have you had this?'

'For about two years. But it's nothing. It doesn't hurt and it's not itchy.' Mitsu sought to make light of her symptoms. In that way she sought to assuage her own fears, but the doctor was busy filling in a medical card in silence.

'Will it get better, Doctor?'

'I think so.' He washed his hands with surgical soap and met Mitsu with an almost drunken stare. He seemed to be sweating profusely. 'But you should go to the university hospital for a blood test as soon as possible.'

'A blood test?'

'Yes, they just take a bit of blood. That's the best way to be sure. Of course, it's nothing to worry about. I don't think it's anything malignant. But it's best to be on the safe side.'

Mitsu's fears were partly allayed by this parting comment. So long as it was nothing malignant. The doctor gave her no medicine, so she bought a bandage on the way home. She planned to conceal her spot with the bandage.

Despite his assurance that there was nothing to worry about, the following evening the doctor rang the bar to see if she had been to the university hospital. He told her that there was a doctor called Tajima at the hospital and that he had been in contact with him. There was a greater note of urgency this time as he advised her to report for a check-up as soon as possible.

There was a slight drizzle in the air the following day. The various buildings were damp from the rain and through the steamed-up window one could see the patients in their pyjamas staring down on the visitors with a disinterested look. There was a crowd of people outside the dermatology clinic, all gazing at the floor as they awaited their turn. There was one man whose face was covered in a white bandage.

Mitsu had never been in such a place. At the reception desk she was asked to wait in the corridor, but Mitsu was terrified that she had come to the wrong place, that she was making some awful mistake. On several occasions, she asked a passing nurse, 'Um ... where ... what is this place?' She showed her the chart she had been given at the reception desk. She then sat down once more on her chair in the corner and started clicking her heels. As she cast her eyes all around, she was occasionally overcome by an unbearable sense of self-pity and rushed off to the toilet. But the more she went to the toilet, the greater her need became.

'Takaki-san, Togawa-san, Maruyama-san.' The nurses were calling out the names in order, but there was no mention of the name Morita.

'I'm Morita Mitsu. Can you tell me...?'

'Please wait a minute. We have so many patients waiting.'

Scolded by a nurse wearing glasses, Mitsu returned to her

seat like a puppy. The other patients all stared at her and smiled.

Finally, her turn came. A light rain was still falling, but she could see a solitary scrawny cat crouched down between two buildings.

'Will you please strip to the waist.'
'What?'
'Strip to the waist!'

There was a stout, elderly doctor seated in the middle of the room and five or six junior doctors all wearing white coats standing next to him with their arms folded. Keenly aware of the gaze of all these eminent people, Mitsu felt bewildered. She was unable fully to comprehend what the doctors were saying. She felt flushed as though she were drunk and asked tearfully, 'Am I going to get better?'

'We don't know until we've seen you properly.' There was a distinct coldness to the doctor's voice. 'That's why we're examining you now.'

Just as had happened two days previously, a light was shone on the dark spot on Mitsu's wrist and it was carefully examined.

'This is an erythema anulare.' The elderly doctor explained this to the junior doctors in a most autocratic manner. 'Look at this. Do you see how the central part is showing signs of depigmentation and has turned white? It's dried up because perspiration has been obstructed. The dark area surrounding it is due to hyperemia. The histological findings suggest a degree of tuberculoid infiltration.'

Their conversation was permeated with foreign words which she had never heard before. Every time one of these entered the conversation, Mitsu tried desperately to remain calm but could not stop her knees shaking. It reminded her of those occasions at primary school when her reflex action had been tested during the course of the physical examination as a test for beriberi. And with every additional explanation from the elderly doctor, the junior doctors leant over and scrutinized

Mitsu's body with a painful intensity, as though searching for a coin they had dropped.

'Shall we do a lepromin test?'

'No, she should have that at the sanatorium. But please do a vaccination test straight away.'

The nurse brought a gauze cloth that smelt of alcohol and a syringe and handed it to one of the junior doctors whose nervous look was somehow reminiscent of the actor Ikebe Ryō.

'Keep your arm relaxed. Keep your arm ... this one's a real coward. Aren't you?'

As he slowly inserted the syringe into her arm, the other doctors stared at the area around the needle.

'Any reaction?'

'No reaction.'

'That's strange. But there are Hansen patients who fail to react.'

When the examination and the tests were over, Mitsu found herself once more in the corridor. Earlier on, it had been bustling with patients, but now it was virtually empty. The man with the bandage round his head had also disappeared. But outside, the rain continued to fall like small needles. The rain beat down ...

The rain beat down. The cat still sat on the damp, dirty ground in the central courtyard.

The rain beat down. On the evening in Shibuya during that first embrace with Yoshioka-san, an equally melancholy rain had beaten down from an equally foreboding sky. Mitsu tried to superimpose Yoshioka's face on to the courtyard. But that face was blurred and seemed to be crying.

> 'Mummy always comes to meet me with an
> umbrella on rainy days.
>   Oh, how happy. . . .'

Mitsu tried singing quietly to herself. In doing so, she sought to alleviate the fear that had gripped her. She used to sing this song as a child when, on the day before school trips, she

125

had made for her younger brother and sister paper dolls that were designed to bring them fine weather.

'Morita-san.' Turning round, Mitsu saw the young doctor who had just given her the injection standing there with a rather nervous expression. 'Can I just have a quick word with you in one of the private rooms?' So saying, he strode off down the dark corridor. Mitsu followed, feeling deflated.

Mitsu entered a room marked Dermatology Library and sat opposite the doctor. Removing a packet of cigarettes from the pocket of his white coat, the doctor stared at it for a while.

'Have you heard of Hansen's disease?'

Mitsu shook her head.

'Well ... we want to do a few more tests. Will you please go to this place for a detailed examination?' So saying, the doctor produced a piece of paper from his pocket. 'There's a sanatorium called the Hospital of the Resurrection about one hour from Gotenba. You don't need to worry about your expenses. We'll contact them and so they should pay your costs.'

'Um ... is it serious?'

'No. It might be a simple skin disease.' The doctor sought to reassure her, but his expression suggested a lack of conviction in what he was saying. 'But one can never be too sure ...'

'What kind of disease is it?'

Once more a look of consternation was evident in the young doctor's eyes. He put a cigarette in his mouth, but realizing it was unlit, returned it to his pocket.

'We're not quite sure yet.'

'But, this Han ... Hansen something ...'

'You mean Hansen's disease? No, we're not at all sure that you've got Hansen's yet. But, how shall I put it? Because there's a slight suspicion that. ...' He suddenly stood up, as if determined to put an end to this awkward conversation as quickly as possible. 'At any rate, please go to this hospital as soon as you can.'

After the doctor had left, Mitsu sat there for a long time with her face buried in her hands. She kept repeating the words 'Hansen's disease', 'Hansen's disease' to herself.

Suddenly the door of the library opened.

'Oops. Sorry!'

The door closed and the footsteps receded into the distance.

Of course Mitsu had no idea as to the implications of this disease. She had no idea, but the very fact that she had never heard of it, suggested to her that this was some incurable condition. At any rate, it didn't sound like a routine illness.

To Mitsu at this stage, the most important thing was whether this disease would persist or she would make a speedy recovery. When she had lived in Kawagoe as a child, there had been a family living nearby called Nakamigawa. Mitsu recalled how the father of this family had spent three or four years in hospital and how the wife had had to work, not just during the day but even in the evening.

She could not go to a hospital. She had no savings and her present job provided her with no insurance cover.

But it's only a small spot. Mitsu tried to convince herself. I've done nothing about it up till now and I've been fine, so....

Having thus reassured herself to some extent, Mitsu stood up and, clutching her umbrella to her chest, went out into the now deserted corridor.

The rain had finally stopped. The sunlight shining through the gaps in the clouds was painful to her eyes. Several patients were taking a stroll on the hospital lawn.

Somebody called out from behind her. 'I think you've forgotten something.'

Turning round, Mitsu spotted a young nurse. She was a young woman with a round face and red cheeks and the arms protruding from her spotlessly clean uniform gave the impression of vigour and good health.

'This is your package, isn't it?' She smiled as she handed Mitsu the cotton bundle. 'Lucky the rain's stopped, isn't it?'

She looked up at the sky. 'Um.' With great trepidation, Mitsu broached the subject that had been on her mind ever since her meeting with the doctor. 'What is Hansen's disease?'

'Hansen's disease?' Naïvely inclining her head to one side, she continued, 'Isn't that leprosy?'

Mitsu suddenly blanched and at that moment the nurse realized that she had divulged what had been intended as a secret.

'Oh no!' For a while, she stared at Mitsu in amazement. She then began to manifest that same look of total confusion that had earlier been evident on the face of the junior doctor.

Mitsu felt as though she had been struck on the head with a great oak cane and just stood there.

'Do take care.' The nurse managed to mutter this before turning round and running off.

The hospital buildings suddenly appeared grey. They swam before her eyes. Mitsu felt the strength drain from her body as though she were about to crash to the ground.

She couldn't believe it. She couldn't believe that she had succumbed to such a disease. She felt empty, the sensation one experiences when, on a rainy day, one gazes at a distant hill that is bathed in sunshine.

It's all a dream. A bad dream.

At that moment a car drove past, almost hitting Mitsu.

Someone stuck their head out of the car window and screamed at Mitsu. 'You idiot! Do you want to kill yourself?!'

The road stretched out before her, a glistening, dark streak like a pencil. With her umbrella in one hand and her cotton bundle in the other, Mitsu stopped half-way up the hill.

As she had done so many times since leaving the hospital, Mitsu glanced gingerly at that dark spot on her arm and shook her head. As far as she was concerned, leprosy was a disease that belonged to a different world. It was not just that the disease bore absolutely no connection to her life. She could honestly say that not once had she even stopped to think about it. Looking down at her wrist, Mitsu strove to recall all her memories relating to this disease.

She remembered the visit to the great Buddhist temple in Kawagoe that she had made one afternoon with her mother. It was the day of the temple festival. Red and yellow balloons glistened in the sunshine and beside them sat an old woman wearing an apron who was operating a machine with her feet and selling candy-floss. Mitsu's mother bought one of these for her daughter and then led her up the stone stairway.

'I told you not to get candy-floss on your clothes!' Every now and then Mitsu's mother stopped to scold her, but then half-way up the stairway she suddenly stopped and tried to shield Mitsu: 'Move over to the right. To the right!'

They both moved to the extreme right of the stairway.

It turned out that there was a man sitting on the left of the stairway begging. He had prostrated himself on the ground, his bald head resting on the stone step. Beside him lay a dish containing not a single yen.

Even when she was a child, the sight of such wretched 'people' had driven Mitsu to the verge of tears. In addition to fear and curiosity, she was moved by an instinctive sense of compassion towards such beings.

Clinging firmly to her mother's arm, Mitsu stared nervously at the beggar from a safe distance. His hands were the colour of clay and looked like logs. They were rounded at the ends. There were no fingers. All five fingers were missing.

'Mum . . .'

'What is it?'

'Give him some money.'

'Don't be stupid.' Mitsu's mother averted her gaze. 'Don't look. It's a leper.'

'A leper?'

'Yes, a leper. If you keep on doing naughty things, you'll lose your fingers and end up like that. So. . . .'

After a while, one of the officials rode up on his bicycle. Presumably someone had informed the main office. The beggar was led away by the official and limped off on his crutches. It was this memory that suddenly formulated in Mitsu's mind. If she were not mistaken, Mitsu had now joined that number.

'If you keep doing naughty things, you'll lose your fingers like that.' Mitsu could still recall distinctly the words of her mother.

Mitsu wondered what 'naughty things' she had done. She

may not have been particularly good, but equally, she had not been particularly bad. In her naïvety, Mitsu interpreted 'naughty things' as stealing, telling lies and other such obvious examples. When her new mother had arrived on the scene, Mitsu had concluded that there was no place for her in the home and had left for Tokyo. And Mitsu felt that she had always given of her best, even when working in the factory. Even when Yotchan had slipped off, Mitsu had remained behind and carried on with the packaging. She wondered which of these was so 'naughty'.

At the top of the hill, she came across a main road with tram-lines down the middle. She had eaten nothing all day, but she had no appetite. She had no particular destination in mind and anyway she had no desire to go anywhere. She just wanted to curl up on her *futon* and go to sleep.

Her mother had always told her that sleep was the best antidote for depression. Sleep... when you sleep, you forget everything, however painful and trying. It was like forgetting everything and quietly dying.

A train passed under the road. Leaning against the railings, Mitsu watched it slowly recede into the distance. She caught a brief glimpse of some students who were presumably returning home from university standing at the train window. The lights at the intersection changed from red to amber and a stream of trucks and taxis set off down the rain-sodden street. This was Tokyo going about its everyday business as usual. Nobody could have realized that the girl leaning against the railings gazing at the train below with that sombre expression was contemplating suicide.

All you need to do is jump now....

But Mitsu was too frightened to jump. She went off to Shinjuku. Since she had no idea where to go next, she went to the cafeteria in one of the department stores and ordered an *anmitsu*[3] simply in order to secure a seat.

Through the window she could see the grey sky and the

3. A sweet dish of honey and bean paste

grey city. She furtively examined the dark spot on her wrist. It was just as the plump consultant had explained to the other doctors: the centre was white as though enveloped in mist. She felt virtually nothing, even when she put pressure on it with her fingers.

I don't care what the doctor says. I haven't got the disease.

Once more, Mitsu began to dig up memories from her past in order to refute this diagnosis. Then she remembered how, over dinner on the evening of the visit to the temple in Kawagoe, her mother had told her father what had happened.

'What! A leper?' Her father rubbed his face flushed with alcohol with his sturdy palms. 'So they still exist, do they? When I was a lad, there were loads of them. They say it's hereditary.'

Mitsu had asked her father to explain what he meant by 'hereditary'. So she could still vividly recall the conversation of that evening.

Of course no one in Mitsu's family had ever suffered from leprosy. Her father was still in good health and her mother had died of an unrelated disease.

As such, Mitsu tried to convince herself that there was no way she could have contracted this disease.

The young girl at the table opposite left her mother and tottered over towards Mitsu. She was dressed in pink and holding what appeared to be a brand-new doll in both hands. She opened her mouth, still covered in food, and stared at Mitsu with an uncanny look.

'Hello.'

Eventually Mitsu smiled and held out both hands to the girl. Mitsu was fond of small children. There was no particular reason for this. But on seeing the children living near the factory, she often used her own pocket-money to buy them sweets.

'I want some more.'

'No. You'll get a tummy-ache.' It made her feel incredibly happy to talk to them in this maternal way.

So now, too, Mitsu stretched out her hands to pick up the little girl with the doll. But then, instinctively, she withdrew her hands and held them behind her back. Mitsu looked scared.

I'm sick. She was afraid that she might touch this charming girl's pink cheeks and those velvety lips still showing those yellow food stains, with her dark spot. She covered her face with her hands and sat there motionless.

'Excuse me, are you feeling all right?'

When Mitsu opened her eyes, one of the waitresses was standing over her with a slightly indignant expression.

'No.'

'You've dropped your bag.'

When Mitsu left the department store, it was drizzling again. The streets of Shinjuku were teeming with people carrying umbrellas and dressed in raincoats of all colours. Amongst them were several happy couples who were walking arm in arm in perfect harmony despite the fact that it was still early. Their white teeth gleamed as they laughed and their rain-sodden faces sparkled radiantly.

Normally the sight of such happy couples would have aroused a type of jealousy and envy in Mitsu. At that point, she would always think of Yoshioka-san.

But now it was more than she could bear to be constantly jostled by this crowd. When the happy couples bumped into Mitsu, they went off without a word of apology. But Mitsu felt nothing. She was exhausted.

She heard the strains of a popular song being played in a music shop.

'That girl I left behind that day.
I wonder where she's living now.'

Suddenly, amongst the crowd of umbrellas, Mitsu caught sight of a young woman she recognized. It was Miura Mariko, her former colleague. Despite the persistent rumours at the factory that she came from a well-to-do family, Mariko was not conceited and had always been friendly towards Mitsu and Yotchan. Miura-san was carrying a large carrier bag, suggesting she had just left one of the women's fashion stores.

Mitsu instinctively hid herself with her umbrella. It was not that she was devoid of affection towards Miura-san. But today it was too painful to be addressed by anyone, whoever it was.

'That girl I left behind that day.
I wonder where she's living now.'

Mitsu was painfully aware of the gulf that separated Mariko-san's world and her own. Mariko was a society lady who had chosen to work rather than having to work from necessity. But Mitsu was obliged to work to stay alive. Mariko would no doubt soon be marrying a successful young man. But even that was no longer an option for Mitsu. Mariko was always happy. She didn't have an ugly dark spot on her hand. But Mitsu. . . .

I hate her. I hate Miura-san. For the first time in her life, Mitsu experienced a dark wave of resentment at the happiness of another. Why couldn't all these people in Shinjuku share her unhappiness? Why couldn't all these happy couples walking along arm in arm wander the streets aimlessly like Mitsu, unable even to cry? Why was it only Mitsu who had to endure such pain and sorrow?

She walked to Shinjuku Station dragging her feet like a woman in the later stages of pregnancy. With nowhere else to go, there was no alternative for her but to return to her tiny cellar of a room in Kawasaki. She had lost all interest in the shops. She thought about all the sympathy her workmates would shower on her when they heard about it.

'Mitchan, it's nothing bad . . . is it?'

'Our bodies are our only source of capital, so. . . .'

'Lucky it's not syphilis. I was wondering what on earth we'd do.'

Mitsu could almost hear their comments.

The station forecourt was filled with the damp smell from umbrellas and raincoats. Mitsu bought a ticket and then drank a ten-yen carton of milk in an attempt to raise her spirits.

There was an old man playing the accordion in front of the station entrance. He was wearing a Salvation Army uniform. Mitsu recalled the crucifix she had received from a similar old man that evening at Shibuya Station with Yoshioka-san. *The God who loves you.* This was the message on the poster that had been affixed to the wall behind the old man. *The God who loves you all.* But to Mitsu the characters were blurred and the message unclear. As she walked, Mitsu found herself wondering why, if God truly exists, He should inflict such meaningless suffering upon such a girl as herself. She wished that she had been born like Miura-san. She wished she were slightly better looking and more charming, the kind of girl who would have experienced no difficulty in securing Yoshioka-san's affections and who would be kind and gentle with everyone. She wished she were healthy like Miura-san, and she would have given anything to be rid of that dark spot. She had no desire to stand there in that foul-smelling lane every night, even when it was raining, attempting to entice customers into the bar, only for them to start playing with her and ridiculing her with comments such as, 'What's this?! Here's one that looks like a pig!'

'Gotenba, Gotenba, Gotenba.' The station official's announcement could be heard over the loudspeaker. No, she was wrong. The announcement was for the Yamanote-line train bound for Gotanda that was just slipping into the platform.

Mitsu was suddenly overwhelmed by an incredible feeling of anguish welling up from the innermost depths of her being. She was acutely aware as she stood there in the drizzle amongst the Shinjuku crowds – as she stood on the road through life – that she was totally alone. Not just alone, she was more forlorn and forsaken than a suffering puppy. Leaning against the wall in the subterranean passageway, Mitsu cried, totally oblivious of the people who looked round at her in surprise. She was desolate. Quite desolate. . . .

The spot on the wrist (3)

The rain clouds hung low in the afternoon sky as Mitsu boarded the train. The characters inscribed on the ticket she grasped in her sweaty hand indicated that her destination was Gotenba. But Mitsu felt as though she were heading for the furthest reaches of the earth. The furthest reaches of the earth – the place where a mere handful of people totally isolated from society and the outside world live together in quiet communion. The cursed disease had eaten away at their flesh, their faces, their fingers, leaving only a hideous form that resembled a wax effigy, but they had to keep the fires of life burning in order to stay alive. Mitsu would be joining this group from today.

'The semi-express train bound for Kōzu and Gotenba will be leaving shortly.'

One... two.... The drops of rain left tiny black stains on the gravel and the lines immediately below the platform. The voice from the loudspeaker betrayed distinct signs of ennui.

'The semi-express train bound for Kōzu and Gotenba....'

The train was surprisingly crowded and a smell like that of rotten eggs came from the toilet, through the door that had been left ajar. The smell of tobacco mingled with the odour of the dank air from outside that had permeated the clothes of the passengers. Clutching an umbrella and a small, old suitcase with battered corners, Mitsu eventually managed to stagger to an empty seat.

A man and woman who looked like a young professional couple were sitting opposite eating their packed lunch. But at that moment, the wife put her chopsticks down and gazed at Mitsu's battered case and umbrella with a look of reproach. Mitsu clung to the handle of her umbrella and cowered in her seat.

As the bell stopped ringing, the train moved off and a greyish smoke obscured the view from the windows that were smeared with fingerprints. They ran slowly past the various buildings of Yurakuchō which were bathed in the afternoon sunlight. As always, the streets were crowded with pedestrians. Only a week had passed since Mitsu had stood on the bridge over the station at Yotsuya wondering whether to jump. But now, once more, as she sat there gazing vacantly out of the window, the mundane reality of daily life flowed past her, oblivious of her feelings. Never again would Mitsu return to this city. Never again would she return to the place where people drank coffee, walked arm in arm, bought tickets for the cinema and dreamt of happiness. She was to be confronted by the world where unending darkness enveloped the forest, where only faint lights from the wards existed to illuminate the fingertips of those whose sight had succumbed to the ravages of leprosy.

As the train passed through Shinagawa, Mitsu sat up in her seat and gazed at the dark roofs of the factories and houses. She was searching in vain for Shibuya. The rainy hill. That man – the first man she had ever given herself to.

Mitsu put her hand to her mouth to stifle the farewell greeting that had risen from her small breast to the tip of her tongue. Once more, the young wife seated opposite cast a piercing stare in Mitsu's direction.

More passengers boarded the train at Yokohama. The number of people reduced to standing in the corridors increased sharply.

'Excuse me. Would someone be willing to give up their seat?' The plaintive voice of a middle-aged woman could be heard from somewhere near the door. 'This old man is sick.'

But the exhausted passengers were in no mood to co-operate and paid no heed to this request. The men opened their copies of the sports newspaper and began to reread them and the women closed their eyes and pretended to sleep.

'Excuse me. Would someone...?'

Of course Mitsu heard this too. Sick? What kind of sickness, she wondered. Whatever it might be, it was nothing compared with the illness from which she was suffering. If he were sick, then she was to be pitied even more.

In keeping with the other passengers, Mitsu too closed her eyes and tried to ignore that voice. Like a barren desert, her emotions were drained. Those who still retain a slice of bread have no right to demand anything of the starving, and equally it was hardly surprising that the starving refused to offer anything to their neighbour.

But once more the plaintive cry of the middle-aged woman assailed Mitsu's ears.

Please leave me alone, just for today. Mitsu clung to her umbrella with both hands and muttered to herself. I'm worse than that old man. I'm tired too!

Mitsu was exhausted. She felt tired and listless, as though not just her physical body but her entire being had been encased in a lead mould. Raindrops beat against the dusty glass of the window and, in the distance, the sea had just come into view. But the sea, too, was dark, cold – and alone.

Feeling the call of nature, Mitsu placed her case and umbrella on the seat and staggered down the corridor towards the exit. Some four or five people were standing there. The elderly gentleman was well dressed and leant exhausted against the toilet door as the middle-aged lady wiped his forehead with a damp handkerchief.

'Um... you can....' Mitsu began to speak, but held her tongue. As always, the sight of someone like this old man had induced a wave of sympathy that lit up her face.

'Um, you can sit down over there if you want.' She ended up saying this and then quietly acknowledged her own stupidity.

'But you...'

'It's all right. I'm still young.'

'Really?' There was a look of relief on the woman's face as

137

she smiled, revealing a number of gold-capped teeth. 'I'm sorry. Here you are, Grandad. Sit down. Don't forget... you're a sick man.'

Mitsu stood in the passageway between two carriages and, leaning against the door, watched the railway lines race by beneath her. The glistening rails. The rusty rails. She recalled those occasions as a young girl when she had carried her baby brother down to the railway lines near Kawagoe to play. How they had placed nails on the rails and then hidden in a nearby thicket waiting for a goods train. After the train had passed, the nails would be flattened like a new knife.

The glistening rails. The rusty nails. Mitsu closed her eyes and tried to sleep where she was. But she couldn't. Grey rain clouds hung over the rice fields and a couple of farm labourers were bent double, hard at work. In the distance, there was a slight chink in the clouds through which the sun sparkled. As Mitsu stared at this, she tried to convince herself that this whole episode of going to Gotenba and visiting the Kamiyama leprosarium was a mere figment of her imagination.

'It's all a lie. Lies! Lies! Lies!' She kept repeating these words to herself, matching the rhythm of the wheels on the rails. She tried to convince herself that she was on a train heading for her home town, Kawagoe. Look! Her case was full of presents for her brothers and sisters. She would spend a couple of days at home, pay a courtesy visit to several of the neighbours and then return to Tokyo. She would have to take flowers to her mother's grave, so she would be very busy. Her father would no doubt be surprised at her appearance after all these years. He would probably tell her about the hard times upon which he had fallen and seek her assistance in securing employment for her younger brother, Kenkichi, in a factory in Tokyo.

The door of the carriage opened and the conductor, who wore an official badge on his arm, stopped in front of Mitsu.

'Can I see your ticket please?' He punched a hole in the ticket Mitsu held firmly in her hand, and continued. 'We're nearly at Gotenba.'

The remark was totally unsolicited, but having said that he

disappeared down the aisle still fiddling with his ticket-puncher.

There was a fine drizzle falling on Gotenba. In the small waiting-room at the station a group of young men and women, presumably hoping to climb Mount Fuji, sat there in their bamboo hats clutching walking-sticks and looking up at the sky.

'We're never going to get to see the sun come up from the top like this.'

'Let's at least go as far as the fifth stage.'

Mitsu watched intently as they took cans of juice and some sweets from their rucksacks and divided them up amongst themselves. She was thirsty, but more than that, she was aware that she had never once been on an excursion or a climb with a group of friends like this. One of the girls in the group, who was wearing slacks, sat down on one of the seats and began to hum a tune to herself: 'Run, Troika. Run Troika!' Mitsu had heard that song before. That was it! This was the song everyone had been singing in The Underworld that evening she had spent with Yoshioka in Shibuya. As the girl sang, suddenly she noticed Mitsu staring at her with a look of envy and gave her a friendly smile.

'Are you from around here?' She looked at Mitsu's umbrella and suitcase as she spoke.

'No.'

'We were hoping to climb Mount Fuji. But we've been really unlucky with the weather.'

'Are you students?' Mitsu spoke cautiously and found herself recalling Yoshioka-san.

'No. We all work for companies in Tokyo.'

She picked up a caramel and offered one to Mitsu. 'Help yourself.'

Just then, someone shouted out, 'The bus is here.'

The bus set off through the rain. In the bus, the entire group was in good spirits and began to sing. The girl who had offered Mitsu a caramel asked, 'How far are you going?'

'To Kamiyama.'

'Oh, they have a festival there, don't they? There was a poster about that at the station. I bet you're going to visit some relatives and go to the festival, aren't you?' The girl appeared convinced in her own mind and smiled again.

After they had passed through the village of Komadome, the houses disappeared and to the north they could see the foothills of Mount Fuji stretched out under the clouds on the horizon. The wind must have risen, because the trees in the groves and meadows on either side of the road were shaking to and fro. At night, this place would presumably be enveloped in darkness. The leprosarium to which Mitsu was headed lay somewhere beyond those trees.

'We're so unlucky.' The young girl still sounded disconsolate. 'It doesn't look as if it's going to clear up at all.'

'It's OK. Tomorrow....' Suppressing the pain that lay heavy on her heart, Mitsu sought to console the girl. She was suddenly overcome by the realization that this girl could be the last person from the real world she would ever speak to.

'What's the matter? Aren't you feeling well?'

'I'm OK.' Mitsu shook her head weakly. 'I must get off.'

The young girl held Mitsu's umbrella as the latter removed her suitcase from the luggage-rack. 'Goodbye. Good luck,' she muttered.

Mitsu stood all alone among the little streams that had formed on the road from the rain. As the bus pulled away it showered her with mud. The young people seemed to have started singing again and the sounds of singing and laughter echoed in Mitsu's ears. She was acutely aware of having been left behind.

She stood still... as still as a pole, oblivious of the rain and watched the bus as it gradually disappeared into the grey void. The wind whistled across the meadows, carving great swathes through the grey clouds and humming through the power-cables overhead. There was no shadow of life, either to her left or right.

Mitsu was overwhelmed by a sense of desperation, as though everything had now come to an end. She was now alone. To be entirely alone was not simply to be unable to meet anyone. She had been physically alone many times in her life, but that was nothing compared with the sense of solitude that now assailed her. To be entirely alone was to bid farewell even to those happy memories of the past.

'Yoshioka-san.' This was the word that crossed her lips as she set off down the road. 'Goodbye, Yoshioka-san.'

Her suitcase was heavy and her fingers holding the umbrella were slippery. Mitsu stopped and for the first time noticed the sign marking the entrance to the Hospital of the Resurrection in the middle of the grove.

A small stream ran between the road and the signpost and a small bridge represented the only link between the hospital and the outside world. The stream splashed noisily against the pebbles and was littered with old newspapers and rubbish. They must have been carried down by the stream from the village of Komadome they had just left behind them. On the other side of the stream the large acacia trees rustled in the damp breeze, and beyond, Mitsu could make out a series of what appeared to be ploughed fields. She could not tell what had been planted there.

Shall I go home? Yes, why don't I go home? A voice kept whispering in her ear. All she had to do was to return the way she had come. She had lived quite happily until today. So why not carry on in the same way as though nothing had happened? Right. Go home. That was all she needed to do.

Mitsu crouched down in the grove, placed her bag on the ground and looked at her wrist. It was probably due to the cold rain, but that dark spot definitely seemed to have shrunk. All that fuss about this! Provided she kept it concealed, it wouldn't harm anybody. All she had to do was hide it, find a new job and....

As she emerged from the grove, Mitsu saw a foreign woman wearing a white nun's habit and carrying a black umbrella.

'Hello.' She stared at Mitsu's suitcase, her umbrella and her rain-sodden face and appeared only too well aware why this small Japanese girl was crouched down like that. She clearly had years of experience. 'Right. Let's cheer up, shall we?' Her Japanese was punctuated with a pause after every word. Then she stretched out her hand to take up Mitsu's case and set off.

'There's no need to worry. Absolutely no need to worry.'

They came upon some buildings that resembled army barracks. This was the hospital.

Initially Mitsu was taken, not to the wards located within the two wooden buildings, but to one of the consulting-rooms. Here she was given a hot cup of tea. As she drank, a couple of Japanese nuns sat beside Mitsu and kept talking to her in an attempt to allay her fears.

'Are you tired? If you're tired, you can take a rest in the next room.' One of them was a young nun wearing glasses and she smiled as she continued: 'After that ... let's go to the wards. We're just like a family here. ... Of course, it's hard being sick, but there's no need to feel embarrassed here. Look at these. ... Who do you think grew the wheat for these hot cakes? Some of the male patients.'

This was the first time Mitsu had ever set eyes on a nun. There was something unnerving about their unusually broad-rimmed hats and the black beads that rested in the waist of their white habits. She had no idea how to reply.

'The female patients do a lot of embroidery here. They sell these for pocket-money. Have you ever done any embroidery? I'm sure you'll enjoy it.'

But for her habit, this nun was no different from the upper-class ladies one sees everywhere. Very slowly, Mitsu began to relax.

'What do you want to do? Do you want to rest here? Or do you want to go over to the ward? All right? Let's go then.'

It was already growing dark outside. The rain had stopped, but every now and then the trees seemed to shiver, showering those underneath with drops of water. Despite this, the nuns set off down the path without their umbrellas.

'Look at these *shiitake* mushrooms.' They stopped and pointed to a small area in the grove where the trees had all been cleared and the ground was covered with brown *shiitake*. 'The patients did this too. And there are lots of other things the patients do. You see that pond over there? That's made by them too. Even those who have lost some control over their arm and leg movements... they still don't give up. So you mustn't give in to this disease either.'

As they emerged from the grove, they came across the barrack-like building containing the various wards that Mitsu had spotted earlier. The building was U-shaped with a central courtyard in which the patients hung their washing. It appeared old and the sight of it weighed heavily on Mitsu.

For some reason, the ward was deserted. The place was surrounded by sliding wooden panelling and the rooms inside contained approximately six *tatami* mats, all of which had been scorched by the sun.

'This is your room.'

One of the nuns stopped at one of the rooms. Beneath the window was a small desk and beneath that stood a doll. Mitsu found something depressing about both the doll and the pink towel that hung at the window.

'You'll be sharing this room with Kano-san. She's been here for two years.... Please ask her all about the daily routine. If you've got any problems, just let me know.... Just because you're ill doesn't mean you don't need anything.'

She smiled and toyed with the dark beads that hung at her waist. 'Oh yes. I forgot to tell you my name. I'm Sister Yamagata. And this is Sister Inamura. The word "Sister" just means that we're nuns.'

The nuns placed Mitsu's bag on the floor and left the room. At that point Mitsu sat down on the *tatami* mat and gazed at the floor for a while.

So this was it. So this... this was the hospital. Here she was in a deserted hospital on a rainy afternoon. It was like the factory after everyone had returned home.

But this was not a factory. It was a leprosarium. And because Mitsu had come here, she was now a leper. Mitsu had realized this only too well a few moments ago when showing the letter she had brought with her from the university hospital to the nuns. But for that, these nuns would not have placed Mitsu in this room.

There was a sound of footsteps in the deserted corridor which presently came to a stop by the door. A young woman was standing there. Her face was red as though feverish and slightly swollen. And there was an indescribable sheen to her face. Mitsu remained seated and looked up at her and the woman, for her part, stood bolt upright in the corridor looking down at Mitsu. Both remained silent for a while.

'You've just arrived, haven't you?'

'Yes.'

'If this is your room... then we're room-mates. I'm Kano Taeko.... What's your name?'

'Morita Mitsu.'

Taeko removed the pink towel that was drying at the window and opened the cupboard. 'I use the bottom shelf... so why don't you sort your things out on the top shelf? Has your *futon* arrived?'

Mitsu hadn't brought a *futon*. She shook her head and Taeko suggested that she tell Sister Inamura.

'Do you mind sharing with me?' There was a hint of dejection in her voice. 'After all, you're still normal, and look at me! This disease has got to the muscles in my face.'

'Have you got a temperature?'

'No, it's not a temperature. My face is red because of the disease. I'm sorry you've got to look at it.'

'It's OK.' Mitsu shook her head. Someone must have returned to the ward opposite because they could hear the sound of a radio. They seemed to be broadcasting an amateur song contest. After a song sung by a man to the accompaniment of an accordion, the announcer made a flippant comment expressing regret about something.

It finally dawned upon Mitsu that it was Sunday. Mitsu recalled how this time two weeks ago, when she had still been unconcerned by the small spot on her wrist, she had listened to this same programme in her apartment.

'Where are you from?'

144

'Kawagoe.... But I worked at a factory in Tokyo.'

'I used to live in Kyoto. I never dreamt I'd get sick like this in those days.' A smile formed across Taeko's contorted lips. 'But ... you soon get used to life here. Oh, that's right. I've got to tell you about the daily routine here.'

The day consisted of getting up at six and then, after breakfast, undergoing a series of tests and treatment until lunchtime. After lunch, those patients who showed only mild symptoms of the disease worked, the men in the fields and the women helping in the clinic or working on embroidery for the community. They worked from two until five and at that point everyone was free to pursue their own interests.

'Once a month there's even a movie.'

'Really?'

'They borrow films from Gotenba. But it's a bit hit and miss, and when it rains you can't hear a word that's being said.'

'What else?'

'There's nothing much else.... But you get used to it. For a start, we're all in the same boat. So there's no need to put on a great act.'

The patients seemed to have returned and there was a constant sound of footsteps in the corridor. Taeko suddenly stood up and closed the door. 'Let's keep the door shut, shall we?'

Some of the patients were cruelly deformed and Taeko wanted to spare the uninitiated Mitsu such a shock on her very first day.

'We can eat in here if you like. You must be tired today, so let's eat here.' Taeko was betraying all the concern of an elder sister as she stood up. 'Right, I'll go and fetch it.'

Actually, Mitsu was not in the least hungry. She felt bad for Taeko, but she could not bring herself to take her chopsticks to the meal with which she had been presented by this woman with the bloated face.

But Taeko appeared sensitive to such feelings. She gazed at Mitsu with a look of pity and then quietly left the room. Once more, Mitsu stared at the floor, focusing on a spot on the *tatami* that had been scorched by the sun. She could hear someone in the corridor saying, 'You mustn't do that, Tanaka-san.'

After a while the door opened and Mitsu was surprised to see Sister Yamagata.

'How are we doing, Morita-san? Have you settled in a bit? I've brought you some food.'

The tray the nun was carrying was piled high with rice, boiled fish and soup. But to Mitsu there was something forlorn about even this.

'Where's Taeko?'

'She said she was going to eat with the others.... Don't worry. She's not upset. She just thought you'd be better eating quietly today and so she asked me to come. Come on, eat up. You must eat. You need courage. Everyone has to fight in this place. This is a place where you have to fight yourself.' There was a look of determination about Sister Yamagata. 'Everyone here shares the same fate. And it's not just that fate we share. But the pain and the suffering. We have these in common too. Look at Taeko. When she arrived here from Kyoto a couple of years ago, she couldn't eat either. What do you think she used to do in Kyoto? She was a pianist. She used to play the piano. She had done a couple of recitals, was engaged to be married... and then she was taken ill. This disease can gradually paralyse the nerve-ends in the fingers and so she had to give up the piano. And her fiancé left her when he heard about her illness. But she is fighting really bravely, isn't she? Everyone here has to fight.' The nun continued with a sterner note to her voice: 'Right, come on. Let's eat. You must eat. That's part of the treatment.'

Mitsu forced herself to eat a couple of mouthfuls of fish. She was usually totally unaffected by the smell of fish, but now it stuck in her throat, making her feel sick.

'I don't want any more.' Mitsu shook her head. 'I can't eat any more.'

'All right. You've done well.... Let's try and eat a bit more tomorrow.' She spoke as though trying to pacify a baby. Then she picked up the tray and left the room.

Almost immediately Kano Taeko returned.

146

'I'm sorry.' Mitsu sat with both hands in her lap and bowed. She felt guilty for having hurt Taeko's feelings. She told herself that she was entirely to blame.

'That's all right. I was just the same at the beginning. After all....' A smile flashed across her contorted face. 'I know all too well how horrible it is at the beginning. I'm not being sarcastic. I was just the same on my first day here... so I know just how you feel.'

There was nothing for the two girls to do to occupy their time. Mitsu opened her old suitcase and slowly put the one or two items of underwear and the handful of sweaters and skirts she had brought with her in the cupboard. From somewhere came a cooing sound as though someone were whistling.

'What's that?'

'That....' Taeko answered. 'That's a turtle-dove. They sing in the trees over there.'

'What do you normally do in the evening?'

'I go to someone's room and we talk, listen to the radio...'

'Sorry.'

'Sorry about what?'

'You've stayed here because I've arrived, haven't you?'

'Don't worry.'

In the dim light, Mitsu stole a quick glance at Taeko's bloated face. The redness seemed to have vanished in the light, but the brilliant sheen appeared more pronounced than before.

The nun had told her about Taeko's past as a pianist. In which case she must have been the daughter of some well-to-do family. And she had been engaged. At that time, she must have been beautiful, just like Miura Mariko. And that woman was now sitting here in this remote hospital with only the turtle-doves to break the silence. With this in mind, Mitsu quite forgot herself and was overcome by an overwhelming desire to burst into tears.

'I'm sorry.' Mitsu bowed once more.

'You....' Taeko finally laughed out loud. 'You're a strange person, aren't you?'

But at that moment Mitsu was preoccupied with a different

concern. The thought that her face too would eventually swell up like Taeko's was terrifying. Mitsu instinctively looked away and covered her face.

'Let's go to sleep, shall we?' Taeko was able to identify with Mitsu's feelings as though they were somehow tangible. This young girl with the plaited hair and the plain skirt revived memories of that autumn evening two years ago when she too had arrived at the hospital feeling, if anything, even more desperate and lonely.

She began to arrange her *futon* with her partly paralysed hands but then, remembering that Mitsu had forgotten her bedding, she left the room to contact Sister Yamagata.

About half an hour later, the two girls were comfortably installed in their *futon*. They were stretched out side by side, but had preserved the greatest possible distance between each other.

Through the darkness from a ward on the other side of the grove, they could just make out the voices of people groaning. These were cries of pain from the more severe cases. Not only was this disease incurable, but some five or seven years later, they too would be transferred to that ward and be obliged to confront such agony. That was their inescapable destiny. After that, there was the small moss-covered graveyard within the hospital compound that awaited them all.

'Are you crying?' Taeko asked.

'No.'

'The really hard bit is not the physical pain. After two years, I've finally come to understand. The really hard bit... is to accept not being loved by anyone.' It was as though Taeko were trying to convince herself and Mitsu was unable to understand the true significance of what she was saying. She was holding the edge of the *futon* in her hands, trying to fathom the depth of the darkness that enveloped the hospital. For the first time in her life she realized that even the darkness gave off a sound. This was not the sound of the trees rustling in the rain, or the cooing of the turtle-doves. The sound of darkness was certainly intricately linked to the sense of being alone but unrelated to this was the sound of the palpitations of men and women experiencing the sense of utter solitude. There was no doubt about it. This was a sound audible only on evenings such as this.

The spot on the wrist (4)

The days blended into one.... For the first two days Mitsu locked herself in her room and refused to go outside except to the toilet. Whenever she heard sounds in the corridor, she sat up with a start and looked in the direction the noise had come from with a look of terror in her eyes, like that of a cornered rabbit.

Kano Taeko did invite her to go out for just a short walk, but Mitsu merely shook her head and declined. 'I'm sorry,' she said by way of apology.

'That's all right.' Taeko smiled sympathetically and nodded.

Of course the nuns too were well aware of the shock that afflicted all patients arriving at the leprosarium. But they refrained from sympathizing too much with the patients.

Apart from the meals, which were brought to her by either Taeko or Sister Yamagata, Mitsu was left entirely to her own devices.

Overt displays of sympathy tend to have an adverse psychological effect on new patients. This disease required not merely a fighting spirit but a powerful attachment to life and the courage to overcome despair. Such qualities could not be provided by others; they had to be nurtured by the individual concerned. This was the attitude the hospital adopted towards all new arrivals.

Likewise, the looks Mitsu received from the other patients were not particularly sympathetic. They too had spent the nights of their first week in the hospital confronting the same sadness, the same anguish.

There was no respite from the rain during the first three

days Mitsu spent in the hospital. When she awoke in the morning, Taeko would have already folded up her own bedding, washed and gone off to the treatment-room and her workplace. Mitsu lay there all alone in the room listening to the sound of the rain against the leaves on the trees. As she lay listening, thoughts of her future and her past continued to spin round and round inside her small head. On such occasions she invariably found herself recalling that Sunday when she had first met Yoshioka-san. She had often recalled events of that day and chewed them over like a cow and she could still vividly recall that scene down to the finest detail.

At that time she had never imagined that she might receive a letter from someone as important as a 'university student'. When Mitsu had shown the letter to her flatmate and asked her to accompany her, Yotchan had replied with a tinge of jealousy, 'Don't be stupid. He wouldn't be seen dead with someone like us. He's just messing about.'

But when the two of them had arrived at Shimokitazawa Station, sure enough that 'university student' had been waiting for them there.

Mitsu had fallen for him on the spot. Ages ago, on seeing the movie star Ishihama Akira wearing college uniform in various movies and magazines, both Yotchan and Mitsu had responded with involuntary sighs, 'Wow, he's great!' Like other girls of her age, Mitsu was desperate for love and when humming a song she would often find herself thinking how wonderful it would be to walk down the poplar-lined streets with a 'university student' just like that.

As a result, when she had found herself walking alongside Yoshioka-san, she had been overwhelmed by a mixture of fear and happiness. Simply walking with a student, she had felt as if she were emulating Wakayama Setsuko, Ishihama's partner on the screen. But then, noticing her scruffy sweater and battered shoes, she had come to fear that she would be hated simply on account of the clothes she was wearing.

Mitsu stood up and opened the window. At the window opposite she could see a patient on crutches being helped to walk by Sister Yamagata. The sky was overcast and there was no let-up in the rain.

The rain... as she looked at the rain, she couldn't help recalling that inn in Shibuya. At that time, Mitsu had been assailed by an unbearable wave of sympathy for Yoshioka-san whose right hand was still impaired by the polio he had contracted as a child. Noticing that he was feeling miserable on her account, Mitsu had felt a crushing sensation at her breast. She had not wanted to go to that inn. But even less had she wanted to be the cause of further misery for Yoshioka-san. It had been raining then too and she still recalled the middle-aged woman she had seen from the window trudging wearily up the hill.

She had one more painful memory. It was of the evening she had visited Yoshioka's apartment in Ochanomizu only to find him gone. Her desperate search for Yoshioka-san amongst the students in the street as she wearily climbed up the hill at Surugadai.... It was then that she had first become aware of his total lack of feelings for her.

Once more as she sat on the *tatami* matting deep in such thoughts, Mitsu cried like a child. It was not just today. Whenever she thought back to that day she had walked up and down the hill at Surugadai looking for Yoshioka-san, she was invariably overcome with an incredible wave of self-pity and would burst into tears. The tears flowed and it was only after she had given herself over to a fit of convulsive sobbing that she eventually cheered up.

The door opened and in came Kano Taeko. Looking down on the weeping Mitsu she was initially at a loss for words. But finally she was able to say, 'There are some breaks in the clouds today. I think it's going to clear up.'

Mitsu turned round and noticed how Taeko's lips were drawn over to the right of her face. She had failed to spot it in the dim light of the previous evening, but Taeko's face was contorted as though she had been burnt and the sheen to her skin was somehow different at that point.

'Are you feeling a bit better? I was just the same. I stayed in my room for the whole of my first week here.... I was too frightened to meet anyone, and I didn't want to meet anyone. All I could think of was happy memories of the days before I got sick.... I bet you're doing just the same now, aren't you?'

Mitsu remained silent, but the realization that this woman had seen through to her innermost thoughts served only to augment her sense of depression.

'I was studying to be a pianist.' Taeko suddenly sat down beside Mitsu and spoke in a whisper. Then gazing at her own fingers, she continued. 'I used to study really hard in those days.... I hardly left the piano from morning till night. It all happened about the time of my first recital. I was planning to wear an off-the-shoulder evening dress for the recital. That's when my mother noticed the reddish spot on my arm and took me to the hospital affiliated to Kyoto University.'

At this point, Taeko smiled as though recalling some amusing anecdote. 'And that was it...'

'What do you mean?' Mitsu looked up in surprise.

'My mother and the doctor stood in the corridor talking for ages. When my mother returned, her face was as white as a sheet. But I was blissfully unaware. So I calmly asked her how long it would be before I was better.

Mitsu suddenly recalled the comment Kano Taeko had let slip the previous evening as they lay side by side listening to the rustling of the trees in the rain: The really hard bit is not the physical pain. After two years, I've finally come to understand. The really hard bit... is to accept not being loved by anyone. Mitsu thought of Yoshioka-san and asked, 'Did you have a boy-friend?'

'Yes, I did.' Taeko's face clouded over for a second. 'But there's no getting round it. Who wants to marry a woman with this disease? I've got no right to feel bitter or hold it against him. But, Morita-san.... We get used to unhappiness. No, we don't just get used to it. Life here has its own joys and happiness. I no longer feel that I have been abandoned here. I feel I've come to a world of a different dimension to the outside world. The joys and happiness of the outside world may be denied us here.... But it's possible to discover a purpose in life here that you can't get outside.' Taeko held her cheeks in her hands. She was speaking not so much for Mitsu's benefit but rather to convince herself. 'You too will feel stronger in a couple of weeks. And, anyway, you have to.'

On the fourth day Mitsu was taken outside the building by Taeko. As she emerged, she resembled an animal timidly reconnoitring the world outside its lair. The rain that had fallen incessantly for three days had stopped and milky white clouds floated in the sky above the trees. Outside the ward, the air was filled with the sound of patients laughing.

'What are they doing?' Mitsu asked Taeko.

'What, that? Everyone's got together in the chicken house. Do you want to go and have a look?'

At this, Mitsu cautiously followed Taeko to the chicken house. One of the jobs performed by the patients was keeping chickens. There was no insurance indemnity against this disease and the hospital was unable to exist merely on its state subsidy. As such, one of the most important functions of the nuns was to collect voluntary financial contributions. Of course that in itself was insufficient and so the more able-bodied men kept chickens and worked in the fields, whilst the women busied themselves with embroidery. The end products were then cashed in to supplement the running costs of the hospital.

The chicken house was an old converted storehouse. There were a dozen or so patients standing in front of it, deep in conversation.

'Come on, Nakano-san. Pull yourself together.'

'Look! It's escaped over to the right!' They were offering words of encouragement to a middle-aged man called Nakano-san.

Five or six chickens had escaped from the chicken house. Nakano-san was in charge and was desperately chasing after them. But because of his deformed fingers, the chickens were able to elude his grasp even when he drew close enough to touch them with both hands.

They were dancing about quite happily.

'There's one behind you, Nakano-san.'

'It's no good, Nakano-san. You have to decide which one you're going for and then go for it.' Everyone was ridiculing him and Nakano-san had turned bright red and was sweating profusely.

'I'll teach you to make fun of a grown man!' He was getting increasingly angry as he chased the chickens in all directions.

Nakano's face was bloated and swollen, just like Taeko's. Amongst the patients who were looking on, there was a man whose head was bandaged and a woman with a patch over her eye.

As Taeko and Mitsu approached, everyone smiled and looked at them.

'Kano-san. There's a circus act starring Nakano-san and the chickens.'

'Really?' Taeko smiled. 'Let me introduce my friend. This is Morita-san, who arrived three days ago. She's finally found it in her to leave her room.'

'Well done!' one of the patients shouted and, with this, the other patients greeted Mitsu cheerfully. Mitsu felt both shy and sad and stared fixedly at the ground.

'What are you talking about? You stayed in your room crying for two weeks!'

'Right. And Imai-san took a whole month. So you've done well, Morita-san.'

They all began to discuss their experiences of entering the hospital. Mitsu gradually warmed to their laughter and smiled.

'Look, she's cheered up already.' The man with the bandaged head and deformed lips pointed at Mitsu, setting off another bout of laughter.

'So Mitsu, you've come outside, have you?' At some stage during the discussion, Sister Yamagata had appeared behind Mitsu. She fingered the black rosary beads that hung from her waist as she spoke.

'Feeling better at last, are you? You'll be all right now. You'll be able to make lots of new friends.... Right, now you're feeling better, let's go to the treatment-room. We want to do a full examination.'

'Taeko-san.' Mitsu looked round at Taeko and, rather like a younger sister imploring an elder sister, spoke in a hushed voice. 'Will you come with me?'

'You're a bit spoilt, aren't you, Morita-san!'

But Taeko seemed happy to co-operate with this girl who had finally come to trust her.

The treatment-room was located at the end of the building. The room next door contained a bath where patients could receive hot-water therapy. Here, the patients were encouraged to place their partly paralysed limbs into hot water in an attempt to restore at least partial movement. An elderly doctor wearing glasses was seated at a desk in the treatment-room and recording something on a medical card.

'This is Morita Mitsu.' Sister Yamagata, who had accompanied Mitsu, introduced her and the doctor nodded and gave her a friendly smile.

'How is it? Have you got used to the hospital yet?'

He had a gentle manner and slowly swivelled round in his chair. 'I want to see how far your illness has progressed by using what's called the photoelectric response method. I'll take a little blood but, after that, there's nothing else that will hurt. So relax.'

The doctor took hold of Mitsu's wrist and inspected the dark spot for a considerable time.

'I see....' His response could be interpreted either as a groan or as a sigh. Mitsu had had her spot scrutinized by a series of doctors in the university hospital in Tokyo as well. These doctors too had evidenced a similar reaction. And like this doctor, they too had looked away, swivelled their chairs with a squeak and recorded something on a medical card. Mitsu sat down on the examination couch in an attitude of quiet resignation. The doctor took two ampules of blood and placed his stethoscope on Mitsu's chest and back.

When Mitsu eventually left the treatment-room, Taeko was leaning against the wall with a slightly nervous expression waiting for her and asked how the examination had gone.

The doctor called Sister Yamagata back and began explaining the situation at length in a whisper. Every now and then Sister Yamagata glanced at Mitsu standing in the corridor. A month earlier and this would have been sufficient to induce a sense of panic and concern in the timid Mitsu. But by now she was emotionally drained. She had already plumbed the depths of despondency. She could fall no further. She was now gripped by a sense of despair and bitter resignation.

One week later Mitsu was at last able to venture into the dining-room, where the more able-bodied patients ate.

Since Mitsu was still able to move her fingers freely and could hold a needle as well as a healthy person, Taeko had suggested that she should try her hand at embroidery. Apparently, female patients whose fingers had begun to shrivel worked on a particular form of embroidery in which they used a special needle that could be manipulated with the palms of the hand. Mitsu could engage in such work in her room and, under Taeko's tutelage she began, stitch by stitch, to replicate a painting of Mount Fuji and Lake Yamanaka.

'That's really good!' Every now and then Sister Yamagata came to the room. There was a note of relief in her voice.

Since the rain had lifted, the rays of the afternoon sun that shone through into the room were gentler than usual. Mitsu gazed at the rays as she sewed and realized that she was beginning, slowly but surely, to adjust to her new life-style.

'Where did you work before you came here?'

In response to Sister Yamagata's question, Mitsu blushed and explained that she had worked first in a factory, then in a pachinko parlour and finally in a bar.

'I see.' The nun nodded. 'We get all sorts of people here. You remember Nakano-san, who was chasing the chickens yesterday? Would you believe he used to run a large clothing store in Shizuoka? And the woman with the patch over her eye . . . she's from Nagano. Married with two children. Everyone has his or her own unique background. But here we are all united by the same misfortune and sadness. Do you see what I mean? It's not the disease itself that makes them miserable. It's because people with this disease, unlike those with other illnesses, are abandoned by the families who had always loved them – their husbands, their boy-friends and girl-friends, even their children – and left entirely alone. That's the misery of it. But there is a tie that links everyone together in their misery. Everyone here shares the pain and misery of everyone else. Did you see the expression on everyone's face when you ventured out yesterday? Because they had all been through the same experience, they just want you to get used to life here as quickly as possible. You don't get that kind of relationship in the outside world. So, depending on your point of view, there is a kind of happiness unique to this place.'

Mitsu may not have answered but she listened intently to Sister Yamagata's every word. Never before in her life had she been spoken to in this manner and, of course, she was unable fully to comprehend everything that Sister Yamagata said. But Mitsu was the kind of person who, when confronted by the misery of another, insisted on sharing that misery and always sought to extend the hand of friendship. So when the nun explained to her that the other patients were doing their utmost to give her a warm welcome, Mitsu experienced a sense of happiness that brought her to the verge of tears. She found herself ashamed of the way she had taken an instant dislike to the patients and been frightened by their unsightly appearance.

'May I just ask. . . .' Placing her work on her knees, Mitsu felt an unbearable wave of sympathy for the other patients. Forgetting that she herself had contracted the same disease, she asked Sister Yamagata, 'Why, if they are such good people, do they have to suffer like that? If they are so good, why do they have to go through such agony?'

'I think about that every night, too.' Sister Yamagata looked

Mitsu straight in the eye. 'I think about that when I can't sleep. In this world the kinder you are, the more it seems you have to endure bitter experiences and painful illness. I often wonder why God insists on testing His people like that. There are some unbelievably well-meaning patients in this hospital. I'm sure they never did anything wrong when they were still living in the world outside. So why have they been made to contract this disease, to be abandoned by their families and to cry like this? That's what I ask myself. On such occasions, there are even times when I begin to doubt the God I believe in.... But then I always end up reconsidering. This misery and those tears cannot be without meaning. They must have some wider significance....'

'I wonder.' Mitsu gazed absently at the window that served as a filter for the sun and let out a sigh. She was thinking back on her own life to date. She had never acted in a particularly bad way towards fellow human beings. Even when her father had brought a new wife into the family home at Kawagoe, sensing that she was in the way, Mitsu had gone off to work in Tokyo. And at the factory, she had gone about her work packing medicines to the best of her ability. Even after falling for Yoshioka-san, she had swallowed her sorrow and left him rather than becoming a burden on him. And yet she had succumbed to this miserable disease. Throughout her life to date, she had always lost out. Mitsu had been convinced that this was an inevitable consequence of her own folly. But now Sister Yamagata was telling her there must be 'some wider significance'.

Mitsu picked up the piece of embroidery she had just completed and left the ward. She wanted to show it to Kano Taeko, who was in the work-room.

A succession of white clouds floated over the zelkova and the horse chestnut trees. A bird was singing somewhere in the dense undergrowth and she could hear a dog barking in the distance. As she gazed at the clouds, Mitsu suddenly lost any urge to go to the work-room. Looking all around, she checked that there were no patients or nurses in sight and hid in the grove away from the path.

She still lacked the courage to escape from the hospital. But she wanted to go through the grove that surrounded the hospital and once more to inhale the nostalgic smell of everyday life – to confront once more the place that the patients here referred to as 'the real world' and which had been Mitsu's home until ten days previously. That was the world in which Yoshioka-san still worked. When they had last met in front of Kawasaki Station, Yoshioka-san had come across as a most impressive company employee and she wanted to return to the world in which he operated, if only for a moment.

No rain had fallen for a week and yet the grove was still wet. The smell of damp earth and grass pervaded the air and, at her feet, the pale purple bell-flower and red *mizuhiki*[1] plants were in full bloom.

Through the trees she could see the fields where the more able-bodied men worked. A couple of patients were walking along behind an ox and one of them was Watanabe-san, the man with the bandage round his head who had tried his utmost to make Mitsu laugh at the time of the incident with the chickens. They were unaware of Mitsu's presence hidden in the grove.

Mitsu could not put a name to them, but there were some yellow-winged birds chirping away somewhat huskily as they flitted from branch to branch. A solitary fly buzzed around Mitsu for what seemed like an age.

Everything was quiet.

But for the grey wards in the distance, nobody would have suspected that this was a leprosarium. Leaning against a tree-trunk, Mitsu filled her lungs with the smell of the trees and gazed all around. Just then, her eyes alighted on two rows of gravestones hidden in the undergrowth. There were two or three white stones that looked new, but the rest were already dirty and covered with moss, following years of exposure to the elements.

1. A Japanese flower of the nettle family

Iguchi Eiji, died May 1946.
, *Augustin Tamura, died September 1941.*
Sugimura Yoshiko, died July 1945.

At first Mitsu failed to realize it was patients from this hospital who had been laid to rest under these gravestones. But when this finally dawned on her, she instinctively clung to the tree-trunk with her right hand and suppressed the cry that had risen to her throat. She had finally realized that this disease would ultimately deprive her of her life and that she too would be buried in this dark grove.

Mitsu ran out of the thicket, trampling on the flowers as she did so. After reaching the white road that lay at the far end of the grove, she stood still and took a deep breath. She felt as though she were looking at some forbidden object. Now for the first time she understood why the patients refused to go near the grove and why the trees in the thicket rustled in the wind all night long as the raindrops dripped from the leaves.

She spotted the main road running straight through the fields in the direction of Gotenba. There was what looked like a lorry in the distance throwing up a plume of white dust from the road and a group of four or five primary-school children walking towards Mitsu, picking flowers by the roadside as they came. This was a mundane scene that until recently Mitsu would have taken for granted. But now it seemed incredibly serene, like an oasis chanced upon in the middle of a desert. At any rate, this was the world of the living. A world with no hint of the disease called leprosy. A world devoid of people with swollen faces and deformed lips.

Mitsu gazed intently in the direction of the white cirrus clouds that floated across the fields into the distance.

Tokyo's over there. Where Yoshioka-san lives. Mitsu stared with a heavy heart. Yoshioka-san. Yoshioka-san.

Some horse-dung and small pebbles landed at Mitsu's feet. The schoolchildren were staring at her and had started throwing things.

'What do you think you're doing?' Mitsu shouted out in anger, in spite of herself.

'Leper! Leper!'

'Lepers aren't allowed out on to the street!'

The children gathered at the edge of the field and, with their hands raised to throw more stones, they shouted at Mitsu in chorus.

'Morita-san, can you come to the treatment-room for a moment?' Busy as ever, Sister Yamagata appeared in the corridor and shouted through the window to Mitsu who was hanging up her washing in the courtyard.

'Another test?'

'No.' Sister Yamagata looked unusually stern. She normally smiled at Mitsu like an elder sister looking after a younger one, but all that had now vanished and she was looking at Mitsu with a tense expression. 'Anyway, I need you to come straight away.'

Mitsu wiped her damp hands and followed the nun, trying desperately to suppress her anxiety. She recalled how at her previous examination the doctor had told her he wanted to determine the extent of her illness. Judging from the expression on Sister Yamagata's face, it would seem that the test had not gone as well as expected. Mitsu sensed a premonition welling up inside her like a dark cloud.

'Morita-san. Where are you going?' One of the patients shouted out to Mitsu as she passed. During the preceding two weeks, Mitsu had grown close to several of the patients with less-advanced symptoms. She was no longer troubled by the deformed faces and the bandages.

'To the treatment-room.'

'Oh, I see. You'll be starting the injections soon, I suppose.'

So that was it. Taeko had to go for an injection once every three days. Now, Mitsu would have to do the same.... At this, she felt slightly relieved.

Sister Yamagata opened the door of the treatment-room for Mitsu. 'Here we are,' she said by way of encouragement.

The revolving chair squeaked as the doctor turned round.

'Oh. Morita-san, is it?' There was a gentle smile behind those glasses. 'Please sit down over there.' He pointed to the examination couch and stared at the medical records. 'Morita-san.'

'Yes.'

'We've got the results of the tests from the other day.'

Mitsu placed both hands in her lap and hung her head as though awaiting the verdict of the jury.

'We used the photoelectric response method to see how far the disease had spread.... But with you, we got a totally unexpected result.... You haven't got Hansen's at all.'

'What?'

'In other words... you haven't got leprosy. Just to make quite sure, we did the test three times. But each time the response was zero. I know how much you must have suffered. But....' The doctor blinked. 'Let me apologize on behalf of the university hospital for the mistaken diagnosis.'

Mitsu felt her head begin to spin. It spun faster and faster and a great blur developed in front of her eyes. Had Sister Yamagata not supported her from behind, Mitsu would certainly have fainted.

The doctor was silent. Sister Yamagata was also silent.

Then, very quietly, Mitsu began to cry. She buried her head in her hands and cried, the sobs growing louder and louder.

'It's all right. It's all right.' Sister Yamagata continued to support Mitsu's shoulder. 'You just cry out loud. It must have been really hard for you. Really hard.'

The spot on the wrist (5)

Mitsu left the treatment-room and emerged into the corridor, still supported by Sister Yamagata. The sun streamed through the windows, forming a striped pattern on the floorboards.

'Are you all right?'

'Yes.'

'All right. I'm going to let go now.'

Left alone in the corridor, Mitsu was overcome by giddiness. No sooner had she recovered her balance than a feeling of joy welled up at her throat from the depths of her being, like water cascading over a dam. Until now, she had experienced such feelings only in her dreams. But now, as she leant against the wall of the corridor, they gradually assumed a reality and overtook her entire body. But strangely enough, she was unsure how to deal with such feelings of joy and reality.

'Heh!' When she did eventually respond, it was with a shriek. She clasped her hair in her hands and turned round suddenly.

'Morita-san.' Sister Yamagata was looking on in surprise. 'Morita-san. Steady now.'

Once more, Mitsu began to cry out loud. Her sobbing reverberated into the treatment-room. I'm not sick. I'm not sick.

As soon as Sister Yamagata let go of her, Mitsu ran down the corridor. One of the patients on crutches who was walking towards her caught sight of Mitsu and stopped in his tracks. Once she was outside the building the brilliant rays of sunshine beat against her brow. She savoured the sunshine and gentle breeze with her whole being. Never before had she appreciated the wonder of being alive, of not being sick, like this. Never before had she fully appreciated the beauty of the sun, the sweetness of the air.

Yoshioka-san!

In the distance above the tree-tops was the blue sky. And beyond that, some white clouds floated by.

I can meet Yoshioka-san again!

She would be able to meet Yoshioka-san again. Once more she would be able to meet Yoshioka-san, the man she had been convinced she would never see again. He had come all the way to Kawasaki to tell her he wanted to be with her again. Now that she was no longer sick, there was no stopping her taking the initiative and going to see him. Like objects flowing off a factory conveyor belt, these were the thoughts that sprang to Mitsu's mind in rapid succession.

Sister Yamagata looked at Mitsu with a look of consternation. Never before had a patient been sent to the hospital as a result of a wrong diagnosis. Even this nun was unsure how to handle the situation. Eventually she asked tentatively, 'Morita-san. Are you going to pack straight away?'

'What?'

'You're no longer a patient, so you are free to leave the hospital. Are you going to pack straight away?'

Mitsu nodded her head enthusiastically. She wanted to leave this world behind her – the world of nothing but distended fingers and bloated faces – as quickly as possible. Those rainy nights, the trees shivering in the breeze, the groans of the seriously ill patients in the building opposite . . . Mitsu wanted to leave all of these as far as possible behind her.

'I'll never come back.'

Mitsu seemed to be talking to herself and a look of sorrow was evident in Sister Yamagata's eyes.

'Of course not. There's no need to come back. I'm sorry I shan't see you again. . . . That's understandable. But will you at least write to us?'

'Yes.'

'Are you going to catch the twelve o'clock train? If so, you'd better hurry.'

'When's the next one?'

'There's one at two and another at three. But there aren't that many buses to the station.'

There was still plenty of time if she were going for the two o'clock. She had no idea where she would live or what she would do after returning to Tokyo. But just at the moment her uncertainty was overcome by her feelings of joy.

One by one, the patients gathered round her. The patients were particularly sensitive to such rumours, and news of Mitsu's imminent departure appeared to have spread.

'Morita-san. I hear you're leaving?' Nakano-san, the man who had been chasing the chickens the other day, limped up to Mitsu. 'Isn't that wonderful?'

'Yes.' Mitsu made no attempt to conceal her joy. 'Thank you.'

'If you're going to leave, you shouldn't hang around here too long.'

'But I'm trying to think where to go from here.'

'You can do anything. I know they say it's tough in the real world. But it's nothing compared with this place.' Nakano-san looked down at his contorted fingers with a wan smile.

At that moment, Mitsu became painfully aware of the eyes that were gazing at her from various windows in the ward. They were the eyes of the female patients. The determined look in their eyes as they looked furtively at Mitsu from the windows that had been opened only a fraction represented a far cry from their expressions of earlier that morning.

There was a tinge of jealousy, even animosity in those eyes. As Mitsu looked round, some of them even slammed the windows shut. Some just stood up rapidly and moved away from the windows. They were unable to comprehend – nor could they forgive – the fact that Morita Mitsu had been granted the kind of happiness they themselves had been denied. But there were also some of the older patients, like Nakano-san, who just stared sadly at Mitsu. Their furrowed brows betrayed all the hallmarks of passive resignation.

'Right. Let's get you back to your room quickly and get you ready.' Sensing the unusual atmosphere that had overtaken the compound, Sister Yamagata was eager to remove Mitsu from the scene as quickly as possible.

When Mitsu returned to her room, Kano Taeko was seated so as to take maximum advantage of the sun that filtered through the window and had busied herself with her embroidery. Hearing Mitsu approach, she looked up and said, 'Well done. I'm so pleased for you.' She stubbornly maintained her smile as she congratulated Mitsu. But the more Taeko forced herself to smile, the more her face betrayed the pain and sadness of one destined to stay behind.

'I'm sorry.' Mitsu sat down on the *tatami* mats and succumbed to an involuntary sigh.

'What are you sorry for?'

'I don't know. I just feel rather guilty.'

'Don't be stupid.' Taeko raised her voice. 'You mustn't trouble yourself with little things like that. We all have our own destiny. It's our fault if we start feeling jealous or envious. After all, nobody wants to be here, even for a day. That goes without saying, doesn't it? Come on, you get yourself ready.'

Mitsu dutifully opened the cupboard door and pulled out her old suitcase. But all she had by way of luggage were a few items of underwear and one or two other clothes.

'Umm . . . '

'What?'

'This is for you.' Taeko opened her own drawer and took out a silver ring. 'I want to give you this.'

'You want to give it to me?' Mitsu looked up in surprise. 'To me?'

'Yes.'

'To me? Why are you giving me this?'

'Well.' Taeko smiled wanly. 'It's no use to me any more. I was going to wear it for my first major recital. But a sick person like me has no use for a ring like this. For a start, the finger I should put it on is all wasted away.'

Taeko looked down at her distended fingers. Mitsu found herself averting her gaze from the figure sitting there in the feeble light.

'Please take it. Unless you don't like it . . .'

'How could I not like it? I've never had such a wonderful. . . . It must have been expensive.'

'Put it on your finger.'

'Really? You're really giving it to me?'

Taeko nodded and placed the ring on Mitsu's battered old suitcase.

Having packed her underwear and sweaters, there was nothing left for Mitsu to do. It was already nearly noon. Before long the patients in the fields and the work-rooms would be returning. Today, too, life would go on in this hospital, just as it had the previous day and the day before that. Whatever their particular circumstances, all had to come to terms with the drudgery of daily life in the hospital. And when that was over, all that awaited them was the muddy graveyard in the grove.

'Are you leaving now?'

'Yes.'

The two girls stood up and looked at each other.

'I won't come and see you off. It's too painful.'

'All right.' Mitsu stood holding her suitcase in the darkness of the room. Then she muttered quietly. 'Goodbye.'

'Goodbye.'

Kano Taeko stood with her back to Mitsu, but the latter was painfully aware that Taeko was shaking slightly. She must have been crying.

It was raining when Mitsu had arrived at the hospital. But now as she left the compound, still carrying her suitcase in one hand, the sky was as clear and bright as Mitsu's mood.

The wind whistled through the acacia trees that lined the path down to the main road and the leaves sparkled with a silver hue. From the shade of a chestnut tree, she could hear the babbling of the small stream. It was here in front of this chestnut tree that Mitsu had crouched down and been discovered by the nun on her arrival.

Having crossed the stream, Mitsu turned round for one more look at the hospital. If that stream were the divide between the outside world and the wretched world of the wards, then Mitsu had just succeeded in taking her first steps back into the world of freedom.

Not a sound issued from the wards. A wisp of smoke rose up from the chimney of the nuns' apartment towards the blue sky. But Mitsu knew the faces of those living within that quiet compound. She knew exactly how they lived. She also knew of their pain and of those sleepless nights.

But . . . that's nothing to do with me now.

Placing her suitcase on the ground at the bus-stop, Mitsu deliberately avoided looking back at the hospital and tried to assume a look of disdain. She was keenly aware of the way in which the two farmers who were waiting for the same bus were staring at her suspiciously.

Don't look at me like that. I haven't just come from that hospital over there. But Mitsu kept her thoughts to herself. Don't look at me as though I'm one of them. I'm not sick. If you don't believe me, go and ask them.

But at that moment, the image of Kano Taeko standing with her back to Mitsu, shaking and trying desperately to hold back the tears, appeared in Mitsu's mind's eye. She pictured the faces of the female patients peering enviously at Mitsu through the windows that had only been opened a fraction.

These were the same people who, until yesterday, had befriended Mitsu and taught her the basics of embroidery. Mitsu felt a pain in her breast, as though she had betrayed those patients.

You must think of me as a bad woman. . . .

As she waited for the bus, Mitsu kept her eyes down and busied herself scuffing the ground with her shoes.

The bus arrived at Gotenba Station. The afternoon sun reflected brilliantly from the windows of the souvenir shops around the square, and the shop assistants were busy dusting the bamboo objects and the packets of rice cakes that had been arranged on stalls in front of the shops. The silver bus passed slowly between these shops. A torn poster flapped in the wind outside a cinema.

Mitsu drank in the air from this world that had been restored to her grasp. According to the station clock, it was half-past one. But Mitsu felt no particular urge to return to Tokyo immediately.

Even after she returned to Tokyo, she had no family and nowhere to live. She couldn't bear to return to the bar in Kawasaki and to her old apartment. She knew that however hard she might try to convince them that there was nothing seriously wrong with her, neither the owner nor the other girls there would believe her.

Mitsu was new to the area and she began walking around the town still carrying her suitcase. The shelves of the cosmetics store were loaded with various creams and powders and there were wax models of curried rice and noodle dishes on display in dirty glass cases in front of a restaurant. Mitsu stared at these everyday scenes in a way she would never have dreamt of before. These were things that had slipped her mind during the days she had spent in the hospital, where the only smells were of disinfectant and death.

Mitsu heard the sound of a popular song coming from a music shop. The singer was Tabata Yoshio, one of Mitsu's favourite artists.

She entered a cinema. It was a double bill comprising *Citadel of the White Mask* with Ōtomo Ryūtarō and *We Are Men of the Sea* starring Sata Keiji. Mitsu was not particularly fond of Sata Keiji, but since she had not been to the cinema for so long, her heart raced as she took out her purse at the ticket-office.

The smell from the toilet pervaded the cinema and there was only a handful of people in the audience. The films themselves were not particularly engaging. Mitsu sucked the peanuts she had bought at the kiosk and sighed from time to time. A baby brought by one of the women in the audience began to cry and a child stood up at the front and tried to get his hand reflected on the big screen.

By the time Mitsu left the cinema, the sun had already begun to set. This little town had formerly been a post station and the streets were narrow. The sun shone feebly on to these streets and from the second floor of one of the houses could be heard the sounds of someone practising the *samisen*.

Mitsu returned to the station and asked an official for the time of the next train to Tokyo. She was told that there was a slow train leaving at 4.48.

Mitsu placed her suitcase on one of the station benches and sat down beside it. A group of people, presumably returning from a mountain hike with bamboo hats hung round their necks and pilgrim staffs in their hands, were studying the timetable. They looked exhausted.

There was a group like this the day I arrived, too, wasn't there?

It had only been a matter of three weeks, but the afternoon when she had arrived at Gotenba now felt like a distant dream. Mitsu remembered the drizzle that had rendered the scene even more wretched and the group of young hikers who had been so concerned about the weather. The girl who had offered Mitsu a caramel. She had been convinced from the outset that Mitsu was a local girl.

That was a horrible day. Mitsu's vocabulary of words to express her own feelings of despair was limited and even the agony of that moment – the sense of having been thrown into the fires of hell – was simply horrible. That was the only way to describe it. As she stared at the dark spot on her wrist, Mitsu recalled the solitary cat she had seen sitting in the rain in the courtyard on the occasion of her first visit to the university hospital. She recalled dragging herself away from the hospital to Shinjuku, with absolutely no idea of how to carry on with her life.

Why was I made to suffer like that?

Why was such suffering inflicted on her alone? Sister Yamagata had expressed her belief that there was meaning behind all suffering. But such logic was too much for Mitsu's simple mind.

A goods train pulled in to the opposite platform. Various names, such as *Tome* and *Shikiri*, designating the contents of each truck, had been scrawled in white chalk on the black carriages.

A station official walked along beside the train, striking it with a metal rod.

'Hey, it's Mitchan, isn't it? Mitchan!'

Mitsu suddenly heard her name being shouted and, turning round in surprise, saw a young woman, with a scarf around her neck, who stood there smiling. Her arms were tanned a golden brown and she carried a golf-bag over her shoulder.

'Mitchan. Have you forgotten me? What's up... staring vacantly into space like that?'

Mitsu had not been staring vacantly into space. She had realized immediately that it was Miura Mariko. But for some reason words failed her.

'Hey, what's up?'

'Oh, it's Miura-san, isn't it?'

'Good! You've recognized me!'

Mitsu relived the bitter feeling she had experienced that day in Shinjuku when she had spotted Mariko in the crowds and tried to hide from her. Never had she been more keenly aware of the unfathomable gulf that separated the two of them than on that occasion.

'I've just been for a drive with my uncle to Lake Kawaguchi. I saw you from the car window. Where are you working now? Still in Tokyo?' Nostalgia was written all over Mariko's face as she showered Mitsu with a barrage of questions. 'Well, I don't think much of you! I haven't had a letter from you or Yotchan. I was convinced you must have got married.'

Mitsu shook her head with a wan smile. For some reason, she felt physically and mentally exhausted and was unable to summon the strength to reply to Mariko. But eventually she said, 'What about you? I could have sworn you'd be married by now.'

'Not yet. Give us a chance... but....' Mariko was beginning to relax. 'I've found myself a boy-friend at last. So life's great.'

'Yes...'

'He works for the same company. It's just a petty office romance actually. But still....'

They were interrupted by the sound of someone trying to attract Mariko's attention from a car parked in front of the station.

'Oh, I'm sorry. See you soon. Take care.' Mariko took off her scarf and Mitsu watched the car disappear from the station forecourt. She felt not the slightest jealousy towards Mariko. She was just vaguely aware that Mariko and she inhabited two totally unrelated worlds.

The number of people in the waiting-room began to increase visibly and two or three passengers carrying pilgrim staffs were queuing up at the ticket-barrier. Presumably the Tokyo train would soon be arriving. A local girl with her hair in three plaits just like Mitsu stood at the back of the queue with a suitcase. A middle-aged woman who looked like her mother and a young boy, who must have been the girl's brother, stood beside them looking anxiously around.

'Make sure you don't lose your ticket.'

'OK.'

'You've got your new address, haven't you?' In spite of all the young girl's protestations, her mother insisted on opening and retying her daughter's bundle of clothes time and time again. She was clearly nervous.

'Don't forget to send a postcard to your uncle.'

'I know. I know.' The girl's cheeks were still as red as an apple. She must have been straight out of junior high school and on her way to start work in Tokyo.

Mitsu recalled her first visit to Tokyo. At the station her aunt had fidgeted with her luggage, just like this mother. And just like this mother, right up until the train had arrived she had kept on reminding Mitsu to take care of her ticket and not to forget her new address.

Mitsu wondered where this girl would be working. She knew the kind of life-style she was heading for in Tokyo. A succession of days in which, determined not to be dismissed as a country bumpkin, she would try to act with confidence. But her every action would be ruled by fear. On her weekly day off, she would go to Shinjuku and Shibuya and be amazed at what she saw. Those evenings spent gazing up at the stars and thinking about her brothers and sisters. Mitsu realized that she too was on the point of returning to this same Tokyo and would be obliged to endure the same solitary existence.

Mitsu recalled the cold little room she rented in Kawasaki. Since she was unable to afford a lampshade, every time the light shook it cast striped shadows on the *tatami* matting. The drunks relieving themselves in the road under her window. On such occasions, the girl in front of her would be able to think of her family. But having abandoned her home, Mitsu had no such recourse. All she would be able to do was gaze at the ceiling, draw the thin bedclothes up to her chin and watch the oscillating light bulb.

Mitsu was suddenly acutely aware that all that awaited her on her return was the same lonely existence. She recalled those evenings the previous winter spent like an abandoned cat with her frozen hands held up to the remains of the fire in the brazier. The trains that gently shook the windows with the cracks covered with old newspaper. The very thought of such a life was abhorrent to her.

But what's the alternative? There's nowhere else I can go.

To tell the truth, at that moment Mitsu yearned for a companion who would provide her with warmth. Not just warmth to her body. She wanted a mother-like figure who would support her head when she arrived home exhausted and lonely. Someone to listen to her wretched grievances. A friend who would laugh with her at the Ishihama Akira movies. All she sought was a friend to remain with her for the rest of her life, a friend who would never leave her. Surely there was someone somewhere to provide such solace.

Fully aware of the folly of it all, Mitsu looked at the various people in the station building. But no one showed the slightest interest in this girl with the battered suitcase standing there with a vacuous expression. They were all too busy buying tickets, queuing up or hurrying out of the station.

'The train approaching platform two is for Tokyo....' The voice from the loudspeaker was precise. Very slowly a grey cab, spewing forth smoke, and several antiquated carriages slid into the platform.

This was the train for Tokyo. Mitsu tried to put her finger on the difference between Tokyo and that hospital in the woods. In Shinjuku and Kawasaki, people would push busily past Mitsu with the same cold indifference as at this station. And there would be others like Miura Mariko who, despite having shared a desk with Mitsu, ended up forgetting her entirely.

The crowd surged through the ticket-barrier towards the train. There were plenty of empty seats. But they seemed to fear that they would miss the train unless they hurried. The young girl Mitsu had been watching earlier stuck her head out of the window and shouted something at her brother. Leaning against the barrier, Mitsu stared at the girl, her mother and her brother. The mother took a banknote out of her large purse and handed it to her daughter.

The buzzer announcing the imminent departure of the train was muffled. A voice from within kept whispering to Mitsu that, if she ran, she could still catch the train. But at the same time another corner of her heart was given over to thoughts of that rain-drenched grove and the hospital resembling an army barracks. In the ward she had just left behind her, the female patients would no doubt be busy with their embroidery. Kano Taeko would possibly be sitting all alone in that bedroom. Mitsu recalled with a shudder the looks on the patients' faces as they watched her leave.

The buzzer stopped, there was a short silence and then the train moved off with a screech. The smoke from the engine enveloped the carriages and wafted down the platform.

Mitsu left the station still clutching her suitcase. Then slowly she crossed the square and walked slowly towards the bus-stop.

'It's Morita-san, isn't it?' A look of surprise came across Sister Yamagata's face as she looked at Mitsu standing at the entrance to the office. 'What happened? Did you miss the train?'

Mitsu betrayed her customary friendly smile and shook her head.

'What happened, then?' But as she spoke, Sister Yamagata picked up Mitsu's old suitcase and ushered her into the deserted reception-room. The red rays from the early evening sun were reflected on the glass. 'Come on. So what happened?' This time the nun stared at Mitsu with a look of concern.

'I've come back.'

'I know.... But why?'

'Well.... ' Mitsu struggled to find suitable words to express her feelings. 'Well....' Then with a slightly peevish expression, she began to write something with her finger on the desk. 'It's all the same ... wherever I go.'

'But this is a leprosarium. A place for the lepers everyone's so afraid of.'

'I'm not afraid any more. At first I hated it. But I got used to it.'

'Even if you're not afraid, you're no longer a patient....' Sister Yamagata looked perplexed. 'This is no place for you. You're not a leper, so you have your own place to live, don't you? There's no need for you to come and live here in this place that holds nothing but pain and suffering.'

'But... but you live here.'

There was a hint of naïvety in Mitsu's voice that made Sister Yamagata look up in surprise. 'I... we nuns have given our lives over to caring for the patients and befriending them.'

'In which case, I'll look after patients too. Aren't I allowed to work here?'

'What are you talking about, Morita-san?' Sister Yamagata got up from her chair somewhat sternly. 'You mustn't start talking like that. It's no more than a passing whim. Every now and then we get letters from female students with the same kind of request born of sentimentality. But as soon as they come here and see the patients and hear their shrieks, they invariably turn pale and run away.'

'I've already heard them.' Mitsu folded her arms on her lap and tried to smile. She could no longer comprehend why Sister Yamagata appeared to find her presence so irksome.

'If you tell me I can't stay, I'll go. But...'

'I'm not saying you can't stay.' The nun looked confused. 'But what about your parents?'

'My father won't mind. I've been living on my own for a long time now.'

'Now what are we going to do? I tell you what.... You stay here tonight and think it over very carefully. That should be enough to show you if it's simply a passing whim. And then tomorrow you'll go back to Tokyo. All right?'

Mitsu smiled and nodded in agreement. Why did this nun have to complicate matters like this? But at any rate she was allowing her to stay in the hospital for one more night. One night could become two nights. And two nights could become a week.

'Where's Kano-san?'

'What?'

'Where's Taeko-san?'

'Oh, I see.' The nun stood and opened the window. 'She was really down after you left.... But she was taking a walk in the fields just a little while ago.'

'Can I go and see her?'

'Of course.'

Mitsu hurried out of the office. Crossing the courtyard between the wards, she knew that if she went down the slope at the edge of the grove, she would come to the fields.

Several rays of evening sunshine streamed down on to the grove and hill like a sheaf of corn. She could see the silhouettes of three patients working in the fields. They looked like tiny beans.

Mitsu stopped at the edge of the grove with her back to the setting sun. The scene which she had earlier viewed with such hatred now filled her with a sense of nostalgia as though she had returned home. Leaning against one of the trees in the thicket, Mitsu looked up at the setting sun and abandoned herself to such feelings.

Miura Mariko and I were married in a crowded Meiji Commemoration Hall at the end of September the following year.
It was a wonderfully refreshing Sunday. Various local schools
appeared to be occupied with their sports days and the sound
of fireworks could be clearly heard wafting across the serene
blue sky into the hall.

The Commemoration Hall was thronged with visitors,
suggesting that we were not the only ones to have chosen
this day for our wedding. The list of those at the entrance to
the hall included the names of more than ten couples to be
married that day. Needless to say, the list included the words
'Yoshioka family' and 'Miura family'.

My brother and his wife had arrived from the countryside
and, as they helped me to adjust the collar of the morning
suit that felt so alien to me, Nagashima opened the door of
the waiting-room, pointed outside and asked, 'What do you
think of all this noise?' In token of our time-honoured friendship, he had agreed to help at the reception desk for the day.

'It's just like a wedding conveyor belt!'

A procession of brides passed along the corridor leading to
the wedding-room, their heads covered in an assortment of
hoods and white veils. It really was like a factory conveyor
belt!

'Can't be helped. Our entire lives as salary men are con-
ducted like episodes on a conveyor belt,' I replied as I slipped
into the trousers of my morning suit. 'Companies these days
don't recognize the differences between individuals. We're all
just part of a package. Even when we die, the hospital dis-

poses of us using the same conveyor-belt system – as if we were mere objects.'

'Come on.' My brother who was helping me dress interjected. 'You shouldn't make such gloomy remarks. Today's a day for celebrating, isn't it?'

'That's right. Nagashima, thanks for helping at the reception desk.'

Nagashima was dressed in a suit and, as I watched him bow and leave the room, I found myself recalling our student days when we had lodged together. The image of our wearing masks and trying to sleep on those thin, hard quilts with much of the padding hanging loose. Those meals of *zōsui* and cheap fish. It was as though even we had acquired a measure of steadfast happiness, however mundane. I would marry Mariko and after the honeymoon would begin commuting from our new apartment. I was determined, come what may, never to relinquish such mundane yet secure happiness.

The ceremony itself was amusing. A Shinto priest with a faint moustache waved something that resembled a duster over our heads as he intoned the prayers. Mariko nudged me and said, 'This is a farce. A real farce.'

The two of us stifled our laughter so as not to offend the priest or our go-between. We were flanked by three or four family members and included amongst these was Mariko's uncle, the company chairman, who stood there, his hands clasped in front of him, wearing a most solemn expression.

'So now you've become one of us.' After the prayers, the chairman slapped me on the shoulder with a look of obvious satisfaction. 'When you get back from your honeymoon, I want you to work hard for the good of the company. As you know, we are trying to run it as a family business.'

These words meant much more to me than the prayers. They were far more effective in convincing me that I was now Mariko's husband.

After the ceremony, we held a small reception and then everyone sent us on our way with three shouts of 'Banzai!' The one who shouted the loudest and with the most enthusiasm was Nagashima. I was reminded of the depth of college friendships. The other guests, including my colleagues from work, all joined in. But there was a glint of jealousy in their eyes at my having married the chairman's niece.

'He's done all right for himself!'

'Things are different for college graduates, I suppose.'

I felt as though I could hear them exchange such remarks as they talked amongst themselves on their way home from the ceremony. There could be no doubting that I had indeed done well for myself. But the reason I married Mariko was not merely in order 'to do all right' for myself. To be sure, there was an element of that involved, but I was not devoid of feelings of love for Mariko. However, it is not possible to analyse love in contemporary society without a consideration of egoism. If egoism is the wrong word, then perhaps one could call it the desire to secure happiness for oneself. In other words, I looked on the desire to 'do all right' for myself as integral to Mariko's future happiness as well. 'What's so wrong with that?' I asked myself.

The two of us left the reception hall for Tokyo station by taxi. We had decided to spend our honeymoon at Lake Yamanaka. We had considered the possibility of going to Hakone or Atami. But about a week before the ceremony, during a date in a coffee shop, Mariko had suddenly said, 'Do you remember that company trip to Lake Yamanaka?'

'Oh, you mean when I showed you all how to ride a horse?'

'You can't call that riding a horse!' Mariko covered her mouth with her hands and laughed. 'You're not going to forget that in a hurry, are you?'

'OK ... And who is it who's going to marry this man who's stuck with that memory?'

'Don't be stupid! But anyway, it's thanks to that horse that I grew to like you.'

Concluding that we owed a debt of gratitude to that poor old horse, the two of us suddenly decided to take a trip around the five lakes beneath Mount Fuji for our honeymoon.

We took the train from Tokyo Station to Gotenba and then,

in a surge of extravagance, we rented a car to take us to Lake Yamanaka.

As we approached the lakes, the mountains and woods were a golden brown colour. Through gaps in the golden trees we could see the clear-blue lake and a solitary cirrus cloud drifted slowly overhead as though somehow etched on to the surrounding scene.

'I'm going to make a good wife.' Mariko whispered this as, having left the car, we walked arm in arm down to the lake.

'Yes, I hope so. I hope you're going to look after everything as a good wife should.' This was intended as a joke to cover my embarrassment. She was at her most captivating and I sensed a shiver running down my spine.

'It was about here that the horse stopped to perform, wasn't it?'

'Come on, let's have no more of that dirty talk...'

'What does it matter? After all, it's that honourable beast we must thank for bringing us together.'

During the three days we spent there, we also visited Lake Kawaguchi. On the final day it clouded over. That evening, we took the bus back to Gotenba.

The leaves had already started to turn in the woods. They were not quite as vivid as those by the lakeside, but the golden leaves fell in profusion on to the bus and the road.

'We came this way on that occasion, too, didn't we?' Mariko took a caramel out of her handbag and offered me one. Her manner at that moment struck me as that of the perfect wife. To me as a man, her movement just then struck me as unusually pure.

'Which occasion do you mean?'

'When we came here on the company trip.'

'Did we come this way?' Come to think of it, there was something vaguely familiar about this winding road and the occasional farmhouse.

'Yes, we did. And here.... ' Mariko was determined to prove her point. 'Don't you remember Ono-san asking about that little building over there?'

'Which building?'

'Can't you see it?'

'That one over there, in the woods... the one that looks like a barracks. And then the conductress told us it was a leprosarium.... Don't you remember how everyone quickly shut the windows as we passed? And I got really resentful at that point.'

I was silent. I remained silent and pushed my face against the dirty glass of the bus window. I was suddenly aware of something stirring deep within me – something that I had long kept suppressed in the recesses of my memory. It was the image of Mitsu's face when we had met that rainy day in the coffee shop in Kawasaki. With her hair still wet from the rain, she had mumbled in a scarcely audible whisper, 'I'm going to Gotenba.'

I tried to recall how I had responded at the time. Instinctively, I had pictured that dark spot on Mitsu's arm. Then, seized with a mixture of surprise and fear, I had picked up the bill and said, 'You're joking!'

'But the doctor told me.'

'In which case you shouldn't be out in a place like this. You should go home to bed. You're sick, aren't you?'

I had continued with a tirade of self-serving comments. Then, standing up, I had merely said, 'I'm sorry to have dragged you out like this. But I had no idea.... Anyway, don't let it get you down. You'll get better. I'm sure they can treat it.' My words may have carried a modicum of sympathy. But, physically, I had tried to place the greatest possible distance between Mitsu and myself.

Outside, it was still raining. Mitsu's damp hair was matted to her cheeks. With a quiet 'goodbye', I had hurried off towards the station. I had turned round just once, but already Mitsu had been swallowed up by the crowd.

Mitsu... Mitsu's in the middle of that wood. These were my thoughts as I sat with my face glued to the window of the bus. The window clouded up with my breath. But the bus kept moving until the grove and that dark wooden hospital disappeared from view.

'What's up?' Mariko leant against my shoulder. 'What are you thinking about? You don't look very happy.'

'Of course I'm happy.'

That was it. I was convinced that I was happy. And yet this trivial incident that bore absolutely no connection with my happiness – this incident was trying to cast a dark shadow on my happiness. I was trying to persuade myself that this was not a part of myself.

For all that, at the end of the year I sent Mitsu a New Year's greetings card. Before marrying, I had never bothered sending cards at the New Year. But things were different now. Mariko reminded me of the need to send greetings to our go-between and others who had helped us at the time of the wedding. She claimed that to be remiss on this matter would saddle us with a reputation as a disrespectful couple. She was determined that this should not happen.

One December evening we were both writing cards. We lived in an apartment in Meguro and, unlike my student lodgings, this was a properly furnished place, with a chest of drawers, a mirror-stand and even some traditional dolls. Mariko was sitting beside me, her white arms emerging from the sleeves of her kimono as she rubbed the ink-stick in the ink-tray.

We ended up with about ten cards over and so I sent one to Nagashima. I also wrote to Kim-san, who had always helped me out with part-time jobs, inviting him to come and visit us.

The next name that came to mind was Mitsu. I stole a cursory glance at Mariko. Mariko was absorbed with her own cards. She was blissfully unaware.

Picking up my pen, I simply wrote: 'New Year's Greetings. Praying for your speedy recovery.'

As far as her address was concerned, all I knew was that it was somewhere in Gotenba. But I assumed there would be only one leprosarium there. I nonchalantly slipped the card into my pocket.

I am still not quite sure what drove me to send that card. Maybe it was that, compared with the happiness I was currently experiencing, the Mitsu I had met that day in Kawasaki seemed so wretched and pitiful. There is no doubt that my feelings at the time did include an element of sympathy. It may have been only a fleeting impulse. But still sympathy is sympathy.

No reply came. To be perfectly honest, it was much better that way. Psychologically, it was much easier that way.

But then one morning in late January, after all the New Year decorations had been removed from the streets of Tokyo, I was handed a letter by our landlady as I stepped out on to the frosty road on my way to work.

When I saw the words, 'Hospital of the Resurrection, Gotenba', I hurriedly put the letter in my pocket. I did not want Mariko to see it.

All that day we were incredibly busy at work and, although I kept thinking about that letter in my pocket, it was evening before I finally got to open it. On the narrow roof of the small building from which the company was renting its office space, I took out the crumpled envelope.

It had not been sent by Morita Mitsu. An unusual name – that of Sister Yamagata – had been scribbled on the back of the envelope, but, as I read the letter, I came to realize that she was a nun who was working at the leprosarium.

I shall not dwell upon the shock I received as I read the letter. But I have to admit that my head was so confused that I was unable fully to grasp the import of even the first page without rereading it several times.

I am extremely sorry for the delay in replying to the New Year's greetings card you sent to Morita Mitsu. I have been meaning to reply and to inform you of what happened to Mitchan (for that is how we and all the patients addressed her) at the earliest opportunity. But unfortunately the pressures of work have prevented me from writing until now. Please accept my apologies.

I infer from your card that you remain unaware of events relating to Mitchan following her arrival in Gotenba. As a matter of fact, the detailed tests she received at this hospital produced a negative reaction, confirming that she was not suffering from Hansen's disease. Such mistaken diagnoses are limited to approximately one patient in a thousand and this seems to have come as a particular blow to Mitchan.

But Mitchan decided to remain here. With her customary wide-mouthed grin, she told us that it would make no difference even if she were to return to Tokyo, and she made no real attempt to leave the hospital. She was determined not to leave this world which is traditionally despised by those outside and begged to be allowed to work here.

To begin with, the other nuns and I interpreted this as either a temporary impulse or else a consequence of Mitchan's over-sensitive nature. As nuns, we talk about acts of Christian charity and we seek to order our lives in accordance with such a spirit of devotion. But charity derives neither from sentimentality nor from compassion. Of course we can sympathize with the miserable and unfortunate members of our society. But we have been taught that sympathy is no more than instinctive sentimentality – that it is quite different from true love, which requires concerted effort and endurance. As such, we were convinced that Mitchan's feelings represented no more than the ephemeral concern that able-bodied people invariably have for those afflicted with disease.

Quite frankly, the reason that, in spite of everything, we accepted Mitchan's request to work on behalf of the patients was because she could be of considerable assistance performing odd jobs in a hospital obliged to make economies with its human resources. (This leprosarium is currently just about covering its costs from the small grant it receives from central government and from voluntary contributions.) The more able-bodied patients are able to help out with basic cleaning duties, but we do all the cooking and meal preparation. Furthermore, the patients are not permitted to take the produce and works of embroidery they have made to the market in Gotenba. Of course, Mitchan began to help us with such tasks.

I feel as though I can still visualize Mitchan working. As I am sure you are aware, Mitchan was very fond of popular music. As she laid the tables in the dining-room wearing a white cloth on her head, she was always singing. At first, one or two of the foreign nuns disapproved of these vulgar songs being sung at full volume. But their criticisms were soon silenced in the face of Mitchan's naïvety. Even someone like myself, who knows little of the real world, became acquainted with songs like 'The sun sets over the mountains of Izu' and I would quietly sing them to myself.

After music, Mitchan's next love was the movies. In this hospital we borrow films from the cinema in Gotenba once a month to show to the patients. On such days, Mitchan would be restless and unable to concentrate on the tasks at hand. Mitchan would mingle with the patients in the dining-room that served as a makeshift recreation-room and it was always Mitchan who grew most excited during the course of the movie.

And yet Mitchan never ventured out to any of the cinemas outside the hospital. Once or twice I said to her, 'Mitchan, it's Sunday today. Why don't you go down to Gotenba? Go and see a movie.' But she always shook her head. And when I asked, 'Why not? Aren't they showing any interesting movies?' she simply replied, 'What about you?'

'I can't. I'm a nun. I can't just leave whenever I want. But you're free to come and go as you please. So go along.'

'No, I'm not going either.'

'Why not?'

'Because. . . .' Mitsu would look concerned. 'The patients can't go outside to see a movie. If I were to go on my own, it wouldn't be fair on the patients.'

'But you . . .'

'It's OK. If I were to go there on my own, I'd always be thinking about the patients. . . . I wouldn't enjoy it.'

In the case of Mitchan, such comments appeared quite spontaneous. At the beginning of this letter, I made so bold as to suggest that charity derives not from sentimentality or from compassion in the face of suffering, but rather that it requires patient endurance. But, for Mitchan, the desire to empathize with those who suffer was so strong that, unlike us, she had virtually no need of such patient endurance. No, this is not to imply that, to Mitchan, charity entailed no such forbearance. Rather, that there was absolutely nothing forced about Mitchan's acts of charity.

Every now and then, I used to compare myself with Mitchan. I understand the meaning of the passage in the Bible exhorting us to 'be like little children'. I felt that God must have a very special love for this simple young girl who loved the song 'The sun sets over the mountains of Izu' and who had photographs of Ishihama Akira plastered all over the walls of her little room. I am not sure whether you believe in the existence of God, but the God we believe in commands us to become like the smallest of children. By 'little children', He seems to infer people who are able to enjoy happiness in a simple, uncomplicated manner ... people who can shed tears of grief in a simple, uncomplicated manner ... and people who can perform acts of love in the same simple, uncomplicated manner.

Not once did Mitchan show signs of accepting the God in whom we believe. For my part, I treated Mitchan as I do all the patients and made no attempt to impose my faith upon her. But there were a couple of occasions when we engaged in frank discussion.

I believe it was early December last year. At the time, we had four children as patients in this hospital. (You may well be surprised to learn that not even children are immune from Hansen's disease, but actually nowhere does the disease spread more quickly than in young children, with their diminished powers of resistance.) One of these was a six-year-old child called Sōchan, and when Sōchan contracted pneumonia, it was Mitchan who nursed him round the clock.

Mitchan's love of children was soon common knowledge around the hospital and she would always devote part of her paltry wages to buying something for these children. Sōchan seemed particularly close to Mitchan.

The disease had already affected Sōchan's nervous system and so when he succumbed to a particularly virulent case of pneumonia, we virtually despaired of his recovery. Because he was allergic to penicillin, we were not even able to avail ourselves of this most effective of medicines.

For three days and nights, Mitchan remained with this child without sleeping. Not surprisingly, after three days she was exhausted, her eyes were bloodshot and I was obliged to order her, quite firmly, to return to her room.

'But I am the only one who can take care of Sōchan.' Mitchan merely shook her head and carried on crushing the ice in the ice-packs. Her hands were frost-bitten and badly swollen and had turned pale purple.

'It's all right. We'll take care of him. Apart from anything else, you can't take any more of this.'

But, in response, Mitchan just looked at me intently and said, 'Last night I prayed that, if it would help Sōchan, I would willingly take his leprosy upon myself. Honestly.... If God exists, I wonder if He'll hear my prayer.'

'Don't be stupid. You....' I reproached her severely. 'Go to bed. You're physically and mentally exhausted.'

But I found myself picturing Mitchan at prayer the previous evening. Since this was Mitchan, I was quite sure that she had indeed clasped her hands together, knelt down on the cold wooden floor and volunteered to endure any pain and suffering in order to help Sōchan. If you too knew Mitchan well, I am sure you will be able to relate to such thoughts.

Unfortunately, the young child died some five days later. I shan't write of the pain Mitchan suffered at that time. Suffice it to say that she shouted out in anger, 'I don't believe God exists. How could He?'

'Why? Because Sōchan died? Because God didn't hear your prayer?'

'No, I'm not bothered about that now. I just don't understand why God could inflict such suffering on a little child like Sōchan. One should not toy with little children. I don't want to believe in someone who can toy with little children.'

It was as though Mitchan were clenching her fist in defiance at the God who inflicts leprosy on innocent little children and who ultimately confronts them with nothing but death.

'Why do people like this, who have never done anything wrong, have to suffer like this? All the patients here are good people. And yet....'

Mitchan's rejection of God was closely linked to the issue of the true meaning of such suffering. Mitchan could never bear to witness the suffering of others. But – how can I explain this? Our faith teaches us that when human beings suffer, our Lord suffers alongside us. No amount of suffering can surpass the despair occasioned by loneliness. Nothing is more devoid of hope than the sense that one is suffering all alone. But even when all alone in the middle of a desert, we do not suffer alone. Our suffering is always linked to the suffering of others. But how was I to gain Mitchan's understanding on this point? No, Mitchan actually unwittingly experienced this solidarity in suffering in her own life.

But I have strayed too far from the issue at hand. And my letter has deteriorated into a series of disjointed ramblings. I have been writing it during spare moments at work and so it is taking a long time to finish. Please forgive me.

Now I have to inform you of a most painful fact. The incident took place on 20th December. We were to celebrate Christmas on the 24th this year and there is a tradition in this place to give something to the patients to mark the occasion. Since we are a hospital with a limited budget, we cannot do much, but at least at Christmas we strive to help the patients forget their disease.

On the afternoon of the 20th I had Mitchan go to Gotenba

to do some shopping. We were planning to take the eggs raised by the patients and their embroideries to a shop in Gotenba whose owner is in full sympathy with our mission and to exchange these for cash that could be given to the patients as pocket-money.

In retrospect, I should have gone myself. But Mitchan was always only too willing to help with this task and I happened to be preoccupied with other work on that particular day. It was past three o'clock by the time she left in our three-wheeled truck with Shimada-san who helps out at the hospital. As always she was humming 'The mountains of Izu' and the patients were all shouting out comments like 'Mitchan, turn on the charm and see what you can get for them!' 'Make sure you don't smash the eggs!'

At half-past five the phone rang. It was the Gotenba police. I was the one who answered the phone. Mitchan's name was mentioned and I trembled as I learnt that she had been involved in an accident and that she had been transferred to a casualty hospital. Even after I had replaced the receiver, my hands kept shaking for what seemed an eternity.

I can still hardly remember how I got myself to Mitchan's bedside. At any rate, by the time I arrived, Mitchan was already in a deep coma. Apparently she had haemorrhaged severely and she had also broken her neck. She was receiving blood transfusions in her arms and legs and a plastic oxygen tube had been inserted in her nose. Her tiny chest heaved wildly like ocean waves.

According to Shimada-san, Mitsu was just crossing the square in front of Gotenba Station carefully nursing the basket of eggs when a lorry backed into her. Had she been empty-handed, she would in all probability have been able to jump out of the way. But since she was carrying the basket full of patients' eggs, she was knocked sideways by the lorry.

'The eggs. The eggs.' Apparently for the next couple of minutes until she lost consciousness, Mitchan's sole concern had been for the eggs. Those eggs, so lovingly nurtured by patients with limited movements in their hands and bodies, were smashed in the middle of the square and before long the surface of the road was a sea of yellow. Mitchan lay face down in the midst of all that egg-yolk.

Mitchan remained in a coma for four hours. Apparently she survived that long only because her heart was so strong. Most people would have stopped breathing much sooner. I made sure she was given frequent injections of camphor, but she never came round from the coma. Mitchan passed away at 10.20 that evening. Before she died, I took it upon myself to telephone the church in Gotenba and had the priest privately baptize Mitchan.

Whilst in a coma Mitchan did utter one cry. But for that cry, I don't think I should have written to you at such length. I do not know the nature of your relationship with Mitchan and Mitchan never made any mention of you to me. But just once, whilst in the coma, Mitchan opened her eyes and moved her hands as though in search of something. 'Good-bye, Yoshioka-san.' That was what she said at that point. And those were her final words.

I have just sent Mitchan's belongings – which consisted of one small battered suitcase – to her home in Kawagoe. As I held her underwear and sweaters, I mused once more on a question I have asked myself several times since that day. If God were to ask me to name my favourite person, I would reply without hesitation, 'A person like Mitchan.' If God were to ask whom I wished to emulate, again I would reply without hesitation, 'A person like Mitchan.'

I gazed at that letter for an age. I have to say that I gazed at it rather than reading it. 'So what?' I tried telling myself. 'I only did what any other man would have done. It's not just me.'

In an attempt to corroborate my feelings, I leant against the railings on the rooftop and stared down at the road below. It was dusk. Beneath the grey clouds lay an infinite number of buildings and homes. Between the buildings and homes lay an infinite number of streets. These in turn were alive with buses, cars and people. The scene comprised an infinite number of lives. Amongst all these lives, which man had not once experienced what I had experienced with Mitsu? It could not be only me. And yet... and yet, what was the source of my current loneliness? I had secured for myself a moderate, yet dependable, happiness. I was not about to abandon that out of consideration for Mitsu. And yet why did I feel so lonely? If Mitsu had taught me anything at all, it was that every single person with whom we cross paths during our journey through life leaves an indelible mark on us. So does loneliness stem from such marks? Furthermore, if the God in whom this nun believes truly exists, does He speak to us through these marks? But still I have to ask, what was the source of my loneliness?

Once more, I recalled that evening in the inn in Shibuya. The walls bearing the smudges from squashed mosquitoes. The damp *futon*. The rain outside. The plump, middle-aged woman trudging through the rain. This was life. And the undeniable fact was that my path had crossed that of Morita Mitsu in the course of this life. Beneath the grey clouds of twilight lay numerous buildings, numerous homes. Buses, cars and people were moving in all directions. Just like me, just like us.

Afterword

Some thirty-five years have passed since I wrote this novel and, on rereading it, I am struck by the immature technique revealed in certain places. Having said that, however, I still find myself drawn to the work with a distinct sense of nostalgia.

Now the book is to be published in English thanks to the efforts of my translator, Mark Williams, and I am somewhat concerned that some of my Western female readers may find certain sections objectionable. There can be little doubt that, in contrast to women in the contemporary West who shape their destiny with their own efforts, Mitsu, the heroine of my story, is too submissive *vis-à-vis* the opposite sex. There are still women like Mitsu in Japan today, but in the early sixties in which this novel is set, Tokyo was full of Mitsu-types.

At this point, for the benefit of my readers, I should like to take the opportunity to say a few words about the background to the story which, at first glance, may appear to be over-imbued with sentimentality.

There is a model for my female protagonist, Mitsu. At the time, there was a leprosarium run by the Catholic mission at the foot of Mount Fuji which, as students, my friends and I often visited as volunteers. In addition to organizing games of baseball, we devised our own feeble shows by way of entertainment for the patients. During the course of one of those visits, I was told about one of the women who was working there. The daughter of a well-to-do family from Kyoto, she was tested for leprosy as a young girl at the university hospital. In those days in Japan the disease was seen as somehow repugnant and victims were invariably sent to one of the sanatoria located on isolated islands or deep in the mountains and obliged to end their days totally shunned by the rest of society. As a result, this young woman, too, was sent to the Catholic leprosarium at the foot of Mount Fuji – only to be pronounced clear of all traces of the disease on the basis of a second, more detailed examination. Just like Mitsu in the novel, the woman was instinctively overcome with feelings of relief and joy and left the hospital for the station planning to catch a train back to her native Kyoto. It was at the station that she made a life-changing decision. Returning to the leprosarium, she devoted the rest of her life to the care of lepers.

This represents only the broad outline of the story on which I modelled *The Girl I Left Behind* and I have changed most of the finer detail. Of course, leprosy can now be effectively treated and there are no new instances of the disease in Japan. But the circumstances I witnessed as a volunteer visiting the leprosarium all those years ago are as depicted in my novel.

Through the medium of this novel, I sought to portray the drama of 'the Jesus I left behind'. Mitsu can be seen as modelled on Jesus, abandoned by his own disciples; she is modelled on the Jesus whom all Christians are guilty of abandoning on a daily basis in their everyday lives. Mitsu has continued to live within me ever since and can be seen reincarnated in my most recent novel, *Deep River*, in the person of the protagonist, Ōtsu. It is my profound wish that my readers will acknowledge the connection between these two novels.

Shusaku Endo